He squeezed my shoulder again. "Why don't we get together tomorrow morning? You can come to my gym and work out. Then we'll go to my place and spend the afternoon puttering around together."

I raised an eyebrow. "Puttering around?"

"Somehow that didn't come out quite the way I meant it." He glanced down at me and smiled. "Maybe it did. One of those Freudian slips."

"It might be fun to work out together. But I warn you, I'm not a jock or anything. Just a little weight lifting and a bit of biking."

We got to the parking garage and he drove inside. "Which floor?"

"Two." I straightened up, peering around the half-full garage. Bill drove up the ramp and I pointed. "There."

An empty slot was available across from my car so he parked his truck and opened his door. He paused, staring at Stella, then came to my side of the truck and helped me out. I followed his gaze to my car.

"What happened?" I leaned over, looking down at the tires. The back two tires were completely flat. "They're totally pancaked! Did I run over something in the road?"

Bill knelt by the back tire and touched the rubber. "They're slashed, Threemie. This isn't just a flat." He looked up at me, his eyes troubled. "Somebody did this on purpose."

# Reviews for JL Wilson

YOUR SAVING GRACE:

"Adorable cats, police corruption, and SpongeBob SquarePants play roles in this novel of grownup romance and suspense. Wilson's characters are realistic and likable. She knows that grownups can be just as insecure as teenagers and she knows how to plot the twists and turns of a fine mystery. The climax is filled with danger and action, and the loose ends are tied up nicely."

~*Lynn Bushey, The Romance Studio*

IF NOT FOR YOU:

"Layla Whitford is my type of heroine. She's freewheeling. She's smart. She's gutsy. She is a full-bodied, free-speaking, laugh-filled woman. I love this character. Ms. Wilson has written one of the most electrifying female leads I've read in some time."

~*Christine I. Speakman, Futures Mystery Anthology Magazine*

# Homicide, Hostages, and Hot Rod Restorations

by

## JL Wilson

**Homicide, Hostages, and Hot Rod Restorations**

COPYRIGHT © 2009 by JL Wilson

Cover Art by *Kim Mendoza*

The Wild Rose Press
PO Box 706
Adams Basin, NY 14410-0706
Visit us at www.thewildrosepress.com

Publishing History
First Crimson Rose Edition, 2010
Print ISBN 1-60154-589-4

Published in the United States of America

## Dedication

Thanks to Kathy for all her hard work
in helping me get the facts right.
We don't always agree, but I always listen!

Chapter 1

    I normally don't go around kissing strange men in parking garages at night, but Bill was the exception to my unspoken rule.

    It all started on one cold spring night when I got to the parking garage attached to the hospital. The lot was full, which made no sense for a Wednesday. I'd been coming for months, and Wednesdays were always the slow night of the week. I was giving up on the garage to go to the ramp across the street when a spot opened up on the ground floor. I shot into it and was just getting out of Stella, my Subaru, when I heard shouts from the floor above me.

    I tugged my winter coat tighter around me and went to the stairwell, pausing by the door to listen. The voices echoed in the cold garage. It wasn't Spanish. Also not French, German, or Dutch. I was fluent in those languages. It was definitely two men, arguing, but the language...Chinese? Asian? There was something odd in the cadence. I knew a smattering of Cantonese and a bit of Arabic, but this didn't sound like either of those.

    I went into the cold stairwell and eyed the steps, then the graffiti-scrawled elevator door. Both were problematic in their own way, the elevator more so. Cursing whatever occasion had made my normal third-level parking space unavailable, I trudged up the stairs, my L.L. Bean snow sneakers scuffling on the cold concrete. As I reached the third floor a man pulled open the door on the landing ahead of me.

"What are you doing?" he demanded.

"I parked here. And now I'm leaving." I started past him toward the catwalk connecting the garage to the hospital but he moved to block the doorway. He had heavy, coarse features, all exaggerated— large nose, large mouth, and round red cheeks. I stared him down, praying he didn't see my trembling hands clutching the strap of my faux Coach purse.

He stepped aside and I brushed past him, pushing open the heavy metal door to the catwalk. The urge to look behind me was strong but I resisted. "Keep moving," my self-defense instructor had said. "Get to crowds as quickly as possible. Don't be alone with your attacker."

"I'm trying," I muttered. I dared a glance back and saw the man coming onto the catwalk. I hurried forward, almost running into a flock of women approaching from the hospital. When I looked back again, the big-faced man wasn't in sight.

It was the first time anyone had bugged me and I'd been coming here for almost two months. The other lot outside was closer, but also exposed. I could park there instead and—

I shook my head. The way things were going I wouldn't be coming here that many more times. I walked through the hallway to the stairwell that led to Intensive Care, big-faced man forgotten as I steeled myself to face the ordeal ahead.

****

Two hours later I was sitting in O'Grady's Pub, rewarding my charitable hospital visit with an Old Peculiar, my favorite brand of beer and one seldom found in any but Irish pubs or the liquor store. The place was jammed but I barely noticed. Sitting by a friend as he died always made my troubles—and the rest of the world—fade away. Billy was so young, only forty. He was ten years younger than me. But AIDS had reduced him to a shrunken old man, gasping and wheezing for breath as he struggled with pain.

"The gentleman at the bar is curious about your choice of beer. Most folks stick with Killian's, Bass or Guinness."

I looked up at the waitress. Her hair was dyed a bright green, the color consistent with the multitude of earrings dotting her right lobe. "Old P is a bit off the beaten track, I guess." I glanced past her and saw a man at the bar eyeing me. It was hard to tell in the murky light, but he looked tall, dark, and handsome. My glance shifted to the man next to him, who was short, blond and ugly. He was also eyeing me, or 'leer' might be a better term. With my luck... "Which one?" I asked the girl.

"Bill Manion. The old guy. He's a regular."

I rolled my eyes. Neither man looked particularly old to me. "Dark hair or blond?"

She set down my beer. "Not Clyde. Bill. Dark hair—with gray."

I considered the guy. He reminded me of Dennis Quaid, the actor, sort of tough but sexy. That was ironic because I'd been told I looked like a red-haired Meg Ryan, complete with shaggy, flyaway hair—not by choice but because of genetics and my own clumsiness with a curling iron. "Well, he may be old but he looks like he's got the tools."

The girl laughed. "You could say that. He's a mechanic."

I grinned. "He could tune my engine any day."

"I'll tell him you said so."

Before I could protest, she swept up my empty

glass and money before moving on to the next table. I had just taken a swallow from the new glass when a chubby young man leaned over me, swaying slightly. "Care to come have a drink with the boys?"

Good Lord, what was this? 'Hit on Mary Margaret Madison Night'? A roar of laughter from a nearby table told me where 'the boys' were. "No, thanks." I stood and took another long swallow of beer. "I only play with men."

He gaped at me, mouth ajar. I gave up on my contemplative night and headed to the door, grabbing my coat off the chair where I'd tossed it. As I turned to push the door open with one shoulder, I saw the waitress talking to TallDark&Handsome.

The cold Minnesota March air hit me, clearing away the fog of cigarette smoke, sweat, and male/female odors from the bar. I fumbled my mitten as I pulled it from a coat pocket and had to grope for it in a snow bank. As I did, the door swung open behind me and yep, Mr. TDH walked out, pulling on a jacket. The coat was short, giving me a good view of his long legs in black jeans and a nice-sized chest in a green sweater. He topped me by about a foot, but I expected that. At five-three, many men towered over me. He had a touch of white at his black-haired temples and his eyes were dark and intense as he stared down at me.

"Listen, I was just joking," I said, snatching up my mitten and jamming it into my pea coat pocket. "I didn't mean anything by it."

"What?" He turned as the door to the bar swung open again.

"No offense, I mean, you're a good-looking guy and all, but I didn't mean you should—"

"What the hell did you mean, you only play with men?" a voice said.

Damn. It was Chubby Drunk. He was swaying, belligerent, and bleary-eyed. He was also bearing down on me with an angry glare.

I am normally a very pacific person, but this night was too much. First the round-faced man in the garage, then two hours by the bedside of a dying friend, then a bunch of drunks singing and shouting, and now this. I put my hands on my hips. "You heard me."

"I was just trying to be friendly. No need to be bitchy."

"Maybe I am a bitch," I retorted.

He turned to Mr. TDH. "All I asked her was if she wanted to come over and have fun with the boys."

"Well, there you are." The man took my arm and before I could stop him, had tucked it under his. "Maybe she doesn't like boys." He smiled at Chubby Drunk. "I'm probably more her speed." Then he looked down at me and winked. "Right?"

"Now, just a—"

"If you'll excuse us, we're on our way to another St. Pat's party." Mr. TDH started ambling away, dragging me with him.

"Wait a minute, I can't—"

"He'll give up, just keep walking." Mr. TDH said this in a low voice as he nodded to two people coming toward us. "You don't want to piss off a bunch of drunks in an Irish bar on St. Pat's. Although you could probably get away with it. You're Irish, right?"

"Not." I glanced back and saw Chubby Drunk being pulled back into the bar by his friends after one last glare at me. "Why would you say that?" I stopped, pulling Mr. TDH to a halt beside me.

"Look at you. Red hair, green eyes, and skin as pale as snow." His eyes traveled over my rust-brown sweater and my faded jeans then jerked back to my face. I didn't have to look down to know my nipples were erect in my somewhat-tight sweater. Cold weather and a handsome man had that effect on me.

"I saw that guy coming after you and figured you might need some help. Can I escort you somewhere? There are a lot of drunks out. St. Pat's always brings 'em out."

His words finally soaked in. "St. Pat's? Damn, I've lost track of the days. Where did the first half of this month go?" I could see the hospital across the street, the lights shimmering through the misty snow. "I was visiting a friend and I needed a beer. Or maybe I just needed someone to get mad at. Thanks for getting me out of there." I continued down the sidewalk to the parking garage, just half a block away.

"Is it bad?" he asked, falling into pace beside me. "You look like you've got the weight of the world on your shoulders."

I stopped again, my anger, anxiety and fear suddenly morphing into grief. "He's dying."

"Isn't there anything—?"

"It's AIDS. His partner died five years ago and now it's Billy's turn."

"Billy?" He sounded incredulous.

"My friend."

"Oh. Sorry. That's my name. Bill."

"Nice to meet you, Bill." I started walking again. "You've done your good deed for the night and saved my bacon. I appreciate it." Some crazy impulse made me add, "And I meant what I said to the waitress, too."

His cheeks, stubbled a bit with dark beard, darkened even more. He was blushing. "Thanks, I guess." He rolled his eyes. "That came out wrong. I'm a bit out of practice with the flirting thing."

I ambled toward the garage where I could see people gathered, talking and laughing, their breath making cloudy puffs in the cold air. "Join the out-of-practice group. Once I hit forty, I felt like I'd been put out to pasture. It just ain't fair, but men get dignified, women get old. That bar is full of thirty-something babes. Any woman over forty doesn't stand a chance."

He put a hand on my arm and stopped me. "Bullshit. If you walked back in there, no one would see the thirty-somethings."

Now it was my turn to blush. "Thank you. But I think I know better." I walked into the parking garage, skirting the small huddle of people who were blearily singing "Oh Danny Boy".

"What's your name?" he asked as he hurried to catch up to me.

"Why?"

"I want to call you."

I blinked in surprise. "You don't know anything about me."

"I know you're smart and sexy and thoughtful and kind."

I almost ran into a parked car, stopping just in time to keep from going headfirst over the rear bumper. "What?"

"Please. Won't you give me your name? Your phone number?" He took a step forward and I started to retreat, but the car was behind me. "A kiss?" As soon as he said, it he blushed again. "Holy Jesus, it must be the Guinness talking. I can't believe I asked a total stranger for a kiss."

He looked so astonished I laughed. "Which do you want? Name? Number? A kiss?"

He leaned closer. "All of them." He put a tentative hand on my shoulder. "I won't hurt you. I'm not a pervert or anything like that. I'm just a guy who'd like to know you."

I looked up at him. His eyelashes were long, thick, and dark, framing his eyes. Combined with his pink cheeks it gave him an innocent look. "Hello, Bill." Grief, fear, and anger all combined to make me throw caution to the winds.

7

He leaned down and suddenly we were kissing. I vaguely heard a shouting, hooting sound and knew we had an audience. Perhaps that was what emboldened me, knowing I was safe. My hands went inside his opened jacket and touched his sides and suddenly he was much closer, his arms around me, his mouth fierce and demanding. I clung to him, my hands slipping up his back as he pulled me against him. My entire body ignited. Every touch, every smell, every sensation raced along my nerves, exciting me even more.

A small thread of sanity intruded and I pulled away, tearing my lips from his and pushing gently on his shoulders. "Thanks, Bill."

I'd gone four or five steps before he shook himself out of his paralysis. "Wait!" He hurried to catch up to me.

"No." I pressed Stella's remote opener and the interior lights came on.

"I need to know how to find you." He got to me as I opened the driver's door.

"Why?"

"I just do."

I hesitated then rummaged in my purse, pulling out a receipt from the hospital coffee shop and a pen. I jotted down my email address then stuffed it in his coat pocket. "Maybe."

He stepped away from the car as I got in. I rolled down the window and he leaned over to look at me. "Good-bye." I put the car into gear and backed out carefully. He watched me drive out of the garage.

"I can't believe I did that," I muttered as I drove onto the main street. "What possessed me to kiss a total stranger? What in the world possessed me to allow a man to follow me all the way to my car then kiss me—like *that?*" Lordie, I was still tingling. I was no stranger to hot kissing but Mr. Bill TallDark&Handsome was the hottest I'd had in a long, long time.

And he was probably the best I'd get for a long time into the future.

The thought was depressing. I inched out into traffic on busy Highway 101, the road that paralleled the Minnesota River on the south side of the Twin Cities. I'd been visiting Billy several days a week for almost a month so I could drive home on autopilot by now. I swiped at a tear hovering near the corner of my eye. That's why I let that man kiss me. Poor Billy, lying in a hospital bed, looking so used up and wasted. And there was that big man, looking so healthy and sweet. "Oh, Billy."

It wasn't just Billy, though. In a couple of days I'd celebrate the fifth anniversary of my divorce from my husband of fifteen years. While I wasn't pining for Jack, this time of year always gave me the Glooms. It also didn't help that in a few weeks I'd celebrate my fiftieth birthday while Jack was probably lying on a beach with that damn girl he'd fallen in love with giving him a blowjob while looking deadly in a swimsuit. I wiped away a tear. At least I got a reasonable settlement out of the bastard.

Plus a total stranger, albeit a drunk one, wanted to kiss me. The thought was somewhat cheering.

I arrived at my small house in Hopkins, southwest of Minneapolis. The village had grown over the years and gradually been absorbed into the metropolis. Because it had been an independent entity for years, it still retained a small-town feel. My street was evidence of that. Tall maples lined the road and the houses were all individual in design and paint choice. Mine was the small red rambler with white shutters on a corner lot.

Major Muffin, my monster tabby cat, greeted me at the kitchen door as I entered from the attached garage. He was followed closely by Sgt. Snuggle, his companion, a petite tuxedo girl. They escorted me to the food dishes whose emptiness I addressed then I plunked down on the couch for some TV, trying to shake the blues the day had precipitated. I gave up when I realized I was watching an Emeril rerun on the Food Channel. I pulled out Paula Palm Pilot and checked my email. To my surprise, I had one from Bill TallDark&Handsome.

*I'm not very good at meeting people and I don't know much about women. But I felt good with you tonight. I'd like to see you and get to know you. Please let me call you so we can talk. I don't type so good. Bill.*

"Good heavens," I said to Snuggles, who had moved into her spot on the rocking chair across the room. "Did he go home to send me an email?" I considered and discarded several replies then went to my laptop on the desk in the corner and typed:

*Bill Irishman: you type pretty good for a guy who says he can't type. Did you leave the bar just to send me an email? Don't you have some more drinking to do? I'm not sure if we should see each other or not. Perhaps we should just say we were two ships who passed in the night. Although I have to admit, I did enjoy the encounter...*

I got up for a beer and some pretzels and by the time I came back, a reply was sitting in my Inbox.

*Can't we meet tomorrow? Meet me for coffee—at the Kindest Bean, on Main Street near the hospital? Can't you meet me? Bill.*

A small voice was clamoring in my brain. I couldn't meet a total stranger for coffee...could I? It was five years since Jack. I'd had a couple of dates set up by my friends from work, but I had not met anyone even remotely interesting. I couldn't meet a stranger for coffee. Could I? With my luck he'd turn out to be married or a serial killer or gay. No, I wouldn't do it. No use setting myself up for disappointment. But what if...would it hurt to meet him for coffee?

*Yes, I can meet you at the Kindest Bean (and what is an Unkind Bean, I'd like to know), but I'm not sure what time. Do you have a mobile number? I'll call you when I can get away. It'll probably be in the afternoon, by two or three.*

I clicked the *send* icon immediately and experienced one of those 'OhShit' moments. Did I really type that? Good Lord, what was I thinking?

The reply came back so fast I knew he was waiting for me. The email had his phone number and a message: *Call me, please. I'll meet you there. Any time.*

"In for a penny, in for a pound," I said to myself. *I'll call. Good night. Sweet dreams.*

*I'll dream of you. Good night.*

"Whoa." I leaned back and fanned myself. "There might be some life in this old girl yet."

Snuggle snorted and tucked her head under one paw, shooting me a skeptical look from one green-gold eye.

Chapter 2

"You're meeting a total stranger for coffee?" Kate demanded.

I nodded. "Yep."

"For cryin' out loud, Threemie! You hear these stories all the time. A woman meets a guy, she thinks he's sweet and he turns out to be a serial killer. The next thing you know, her body parts are found in a chipper/shredder somewhere!"

Kate Jacobs and I sat at a table in the company lunchroom, unpacking our brown bag lunches. Kate's contained a sandwich and some raw veggies. Mine had an apple and a blob of peanut butter in a plastic container. "That's it for lunch?" she asked.

I nodded. "I already ate the raw veggies and the jell-o. I got hungry."

"You're determined to lose weight, aren't you?" Kate asked.

I sliced the apple and smeared it with peanut butter. "I *will* lose five more pounds by my fiftieth birthday. And I *will* wear a swimsuit. Even if I make people retch with disgust, I *will* wear a swimsuit."

Kate shook her head. "I don't know why you don't believe me when I say that your 49.99-year-old body looks fine." She pointed a celery stick at me. "Remember when we went shopping and you tried on that little yellow swimsuit with the big green polka dots? You were a hot babe."

"Five pounds," I mumbled around a bite of apple. "Just five more pounds." Kate couldn't understand. She was five-six and weighed about one hundred pounds. I, on the other hand, was five-three and weighed one-hundred-thirty. Those five pounds were critical.

"I can't convince you of your babeness, can I?"

I shook my head.

"Okay, then let's return to the topic at hand. You can't meet a serial killer for coffee."

"He's not a serial killer."

"How do you know? Do you know what a serial killer looks like?"

"Even if he looked like a serial killer, that doesn't mean he is one." I waved my knife, and peanut butter landed precariously on my apple. "Bruce Springsteen looks like a serial killer on some of his album covers and I'd meet Bruce for coffee. Eric Clapton looked like a serial killer when he was with Cream and as you know I'd meet Eric in a dark alley for any reason whatsoever."

Kate rolled her eyes. "Just throw Paul McCartney in and make it the Holy Trinity."

I wrinkled my nose. "Neil Young, maybe. Not Paul. He's too cute."

"Whatever." Kate waved that away with a ladylike sweep of her celery. "You can't meet this man for coffee. Good heavens, what if he steals you away for some nefarious purpose?"

I remembered Bill TallDark&Handsome's dark, smoldering eyes. "Okay. He can."

"Threemie!" Kate looked up as Ken Madison, a co-worker, sauntered over to our table. "You tell her, Ken. She can't meet a total stranger for coffee."

Ken was in his mid-thirties, with broad, plain features, and skin the color of burnished walnut. He peered down at me, a worried smile creasing his dark face. "You're meeting a stranger for coffee? Do you think you should?" He looked at my lunch. "Are you still worried about losing weight?"

"I'm not worried. It's just a goal I've set for myself. *Lose 20 pounds. Lower your golf handicap to 12. Eat more fruit.* A goal." I ran a hand through my hair, pushing it behind my ears. Like weight loss, I had a hair goal: figure out a hairstyle before I died. I was currently on the 'chin-length and too straight and thick to do anything with it' phase.

"Men don't like dieting women," Ken pointed out.

I sighed. I was the only person in the Publications department who wasn't married or living with someone. My co-workers saw that as a challenge. Ken and his wife often invited me over for dinner with *a really great guy we know.* Kate and her partner Martha looked for brothers of gay friends to fix me up with. So far, no one had clicked. "It's a public coffee shop in the middle of a town, for cryin' out loud." I smeared the last of my peanut butter on the apple. "I'll visit Billy after I see this guy."

Silence hung over the table. "I can't go, Threemie," Kate said. "I just can't do it."

I heard the guilt in her voice. "He understands." I stared down at the remains of my lunch. "It won't be long now."

"Aw, shit," Ken said, his face bleak. "I didn't know it was that close."

"His brother is there. They're talking about taking him off the meds today or tomorrow. They'll just leave the morphine in."

"Oh, man," Kate said, hiding her eyes with one hand. Kate, Billy, and I had worked together for ten years. Kate had been a tireless visitor to Billy's house when he'd been laid low with the various illnesses that plagued him in the last year. It was only in the past week or two she'd lost her courage and couldn't face him anymore. "I can't go through it again," Kate said. "First Garth, then Mom, and now Billy. I can't go through it again."

I nodded. Garth had been Billy's partner. His death was hard on everyone because Billy took it so hard. Then Kate's mother died suddenly of a heart attack. Now Billy was sick and dying. "Billy won't know. I'll tell him you love him." I wiped at a tear as I squeezed Kate's shoulder.

"I'm worried about you," she said, covering my hand with hers. "I'm worried about you and this serial killer."

"Serial killer?" Ken asked.

"Oh, for heaven's sake, I'm having a cup of coffee with the guy." I glanced at my Timex. "But if I don't get back to work, I won't have time to meet him, so I need to go." I wadded up my napkin and lobbed it toward the wastebasket, scoring a perfect shot.

"Still..." Kate started.

"It's handled," I said, more confidently than I felt.

As I sat in my last meeting of the day, I considered Kate's concerns. I knew I should be more worried but somehow I just couldn't be. I remembered Bill's flustered, earnest look. He looked trustworthy and he acted like it. Heavens, he could've mugged me but he didn't. He'd been a gentleman. Except for that kiss.

My heart sort of skipped as I remembered that incendiary kiss. If he made love the way he kissed... I shook myself out of that erotic daydream before I could make a fool of myself in public. It was a long way from a kiss to making love. I'd be content to start with a cup of coffee and see where it went.

When the meeting broke up, I hurried back to my cube, grabbed my purse and coat, and went out the door, dialing my cell phone as I walked.

He answered on the first ring. "This is Bill."

I slung my purse into Stella's passenger seat. "I'm on my way, Bill. I'll be there in twenty minutes or so."

"I'll be waiting—" He hesitated. "What's your name?"

"Mary. But everybody calls me Threemie."

"Threemie?" He tried out my nickname slowly. "What's that mean?"

"I'll explain when I see you. Save me a seat."

"Okay. Threemie?"

"Hmm?" I fumbled with the phone and my seat belt.

"Thanks for taking a chance." He hung up before I could reply. I closed the phone thoughtfully. Sweet and smart. A nice combination.

I nabbed a spot on the second floor of the parking garage. As I walked to the stairwell I saw yellow official-looking tape roping off a portion of the third floor of the parking garage. Orange cones prevented anyone from going into that part, directing traffic beyond to the ramp leading upward. I hurried down the steps, emerging onto the sidewalk on the side of the building facing the small downtown district. I saw Bill immediately. He stood under the awning at the Kindest Bean Coffee Shop, looking around. I paused in the shadows of the parking garage to examine him.

He was, indeed, tall, dark, and handsome. In the bright March daylight I could easily see the white highlights in his black hair at his temple and near his ears. His long, oval face was shadowed with beard and his eyes were that marvelous deep blue color, a sharp contrast to his pale skin.

Bill looked around, his eyes searching. When I

stepped out of the shadows, his face lit up. He smiled and waved. Most men would've shown a studied indifference or casualness but he looked pleased to see me. "Hey there," I called out as I neared him.

He looked down at me, his intense gaze almost overwhelming. "I thought you might not show up," he said, leaning on the doorjamb and smiling.

"I told you I'd be here."

"I know but...I thought I might have dreamed you." He gestured me to precede him into the small coffee shop and I did, glad he couldn't see my stupid grin at his words.

We sat at a small table on the far side of the shop. I pulled off my mittens, setting them on the table. He looked at my hands then blurted, "I didn't even think to ask. You're not married, are you?"

"No, I'm not married." I looked up as a waitress approached us. "Coffee."

"What kind? We've got imported Columbian, dark roast and—"

"Coffee. Folgers if you have it, otherwise it doesn't matter. With cream and sugar." I had no knowledge of exotic coffees nor did I care to learn.

Bill smiled. "Make it two."

The waitress rolled her eyes and walked away, her slouching posture advertising the fact she had two losers for customers. Bill shrugged out of his jacket and draped it over an adjacent chair. "I wasn't sure. About if you were married."

"I wouldn't be here if I were."

He looked uncomfortable. "I wasn't sure."

"I wouldn't be. I believe marriage vows are vows."

He swallowed so hard I saw his Adam's apple bob. "So do I."

"You aren't married?"

"No, I was kind of engaged once but she decided she didn't want to get married."

"That's a shocker," I teased. "You seem like a good catch."

He looked embarrassed. "Nah. I'm just a guy."

The waitress plunked down two mugs and creamers in little tubs in a chipped dish, leaving a carafe on the table. I poured two mugs of coffee. "Of course, I don't know you well at all. All we shared was one kiss."

Bill's face flooded red with color. "I don't know what came over me. I don't usually go around asking women to kiss me like that." He sipped at the scalding coffee.

I put a restraining hand on his arm. "Wait for it to cool down, Bill."

He looked at me, his eyes wide. "What?"

"The coffee."

He looked down at the coffee mug then to my hand on his arm. He wore a red sweater with a red plaid shirt underneath it and my pale, chapped hand contrasted with the dark red fabric. "Oh."

"So what do you do for a living, Bill, that you can drop everything and come meet a strange woman for coffee?"

He put his free hand over mine. "I'm retired."

"You're too young to be retired." I reluctantly slid my hand out from underneath his. His rough, callused palm felt good.

"Nope. I got my thirty years in then worked for a couple more years and realized it just wasn't much fun anymore." He scowled down at his coffee, some memory apparently making him unhappy.

"You must have started working when you were a child." I was teasing but he looked so gratified I was glad he didn't realize it.

"I started at the factory when I got back from 'Nam."

"Well, you're a young-looking retiree. And a hip one. That email last night was cool."

"It was, wasn't it?" Then he reddened again. "I'd like to get email to use at home. I went to the library last night to use their terminals."

He'd sought out a terminal at the library in order to send me email? Impressive. "Don't you have a computer at home?"

"I have one in my workshop, but it's kind of beat up." He sipped the coffee. "I should get one of those email things."

"Spend the money and get a good computer."

His dark blue eyes seemed to drink me in. "Do you know about computers?"

I smiled. "Yeah. I work for a computer company."

"You've probably got a computer science degree, hunh?"

I hesitated. This was always tricky. "Yeah."

"More than one?" he asked, sipping his coffee.

"Hmm. So where did you retire from?"

"The John Deere factory. I ran the machine shop. You were going to explain your name."

"It's my initials. Three 'M's: Mary Margaret Madison." Then I realized what I'd said. I shouldn't have given him my full name. Oh well; too late now. "My brother started the nickname when I was little." I remembered Bill's email address. "What about you, Mr. Wam52?"

"Wam? Oh, that. It's just my initials. William Albert Manion." He fiddled with a creamer tub. "Would you help me figure out what kind of computer to get so I could have email at home? My sister lives in Georgia and email would be a good way to stay in touch."

"Sure. I'm always willing to spend someone else's money." I grinned at him. Bill smiled, revealing two deep dimples at the sides of his mouth.

"How about this weekend? Maybe on Saturday? We could go shopping for a computer then maybe go out for dinner or something." Bill glanced at me from under his lashes then continued fiddling with the creamer.

"That sounds like fun."

He blew out a shaky breath. "Good," he said, his dark navy eyes meeting mine. "I'm out of practice with asking women out. I wasn't sure what you'd say."

I blinked at the intensity of his gaze. My heart began its erratic thudding again and I almost spilled my coffee as I sipped. Dinner or something? Yeah. That would be nice. "I say yes. So what are you doing with your retirement, Bill?"

He began to talk about the car he was restoring. I saw the excitement in his eyes as he described paint chips, upholstery matching, and the search for spare parts. "You can't just buy reproduction stuff. I'm aiming for a street-show quality restoration and I can't use repro stuff."

"I'll bet there's a bunch of information online about it." I hadn't even known such a hobby existed. It was fascinating.

He refilled his mug, then mine. "There is. I've done a bit of research on it, but I'm sure I could do more. Maybe you could help me with that, too."

Why wasn't this guy roped and hogtied? He was handsome, sexy, and sweet...what the hell was the deal? I felt a brief stirring of concern but banished it immediately. One woman's loss is another woman's gain. I wasn't going to let unfounded worry shape my opinion.

"You're easy to talk to," he blurted. "Most women don't care about cars." He frowned into his mug. "I dated a woman once who said it was boring. I guess it is."

I put a hand on his, squeezing gently. "I'd like to see the cars you're working on."

His head snapped up. "Really?"

"It sounds interesting. I do a lot of gardening and that's boring to a lot of people."

Our gazes met and held. "I don't know much about gardening," he finally said, tearing his eyes away from mine. "I'll bet there's a lot to know."

"I like to cook, too. Maybe I'll make us lunch."

"Would you?" I nodded. He hesitated then asked, "Where do you live, Threemie? Do you have a big garden?"

I started talking and the next time I noticed, it was getting dark outside. The five o'clock news was just starting on the TV monitor above the espresso machine. The lead reporter, a handsome man with wavy gray hair, was saying, "...no further developments in the murder that occurred last night in the downtown district of a nearby suburb."

"That's the story about the murder," Bill said. "The one last night."

I looked around, surprised by the passage of time and the existence of other people. I was totally involved in our conversation. "What murder?" I peered at the TV monitor, unable to hear much over the buzz of voices.

"Somebody was killed in that parking lot last night." Bill nodded toward the window and the garage where I'd parked. "They found the body this morning."

"That explains the yellow tape I saw over there. Who was it?"

"A cop. It was somebody working undercover." Bill caught the eye of the frowning waitress. "I think we've outstayed our welcome."

I followed his gaze. "Probably. A good tip will go a long way to making things right, though." I reached for my purse but Bill beat me to it, laying a twenty-dollar bill on the table. "Hey, this is Dutch treat," I protested.

"Nope. It's my treat. I was rude to you last

night." He smiled at me, those dimples once again appearing. "Do you forgive me?"

I gave him a considering look. "You are such a flirt."

His eyes widened with surprise. "Really?"

"Really. And yes, I forgive you." I got up and started to pull on my coat but Bill was on his feet, holding it for me so I could slip my arms into the sleeves. "And you're such a gentleman." I looked up at him over my shoulder. "What time should we meet on Saturday for the shopping event?"

"I can pick you up." Bill shrugged into his jacket and walked with me to the door.

I smiled apologetically. "I think we should meet somewhere. I trust you. But..."

He looked puzzled for a minute then said, "No, you're right. It pays to be careful. You don't know anything about me. You name the place and we'll meet."

"How about here? Let's meet here at noon. How's that?"

"That works fine."

I stood on my tiptoes and kissed him on the cheek, my hands on his shoulders to maintain balance. "Thanks, Bill."

He touched my cheek. "It was my pleasure."

"Not for the coffee. For being you." I kissed him again, this time a lingering kiss on the lips. "See you on Saturday." I hurried out, glancing back once to see him staring after me as I went across the street to the hospital.

I felt lighter than air. *I had a date!* A date with an unmarried, handsome, non-gay guy! I paused in the crosswalk, almost getting run down before I noticed the light had changed. I was pretty darn sure he was non-gay. The way he looked me over told me he appreciated what he saw. I thanked the Fashion Gods who had prompted me to wear my nicest jeans and pale green sweater today. Both were new acquisitions to celebrate my descent to a size ten and they were a bit snug. I was sure Bill noticed.

I passed through the hospital lobby, skirting the elevator and heading for the stairwell. As I trudged up the stairs I pondered the workings of Fate. Go figure. Who would have thought a guy like Bill "WAM" Manion would fall into my lap? I hoped he was going to fall, anyway. I had a brief moment of hesitation when I thought of my less-than-svelte body, but I decided not to let it bug me and allowed my fantasies to take flight. By the time I got to the fourth floor, I was out of breath and hot and it wasn't just from the exercise. I have a good imagination and I gave it free rein as I walked through the maze of corridors to the ICU.

Billy was sleeping when I got to his room, so I chatted with Mark, his brother, then sat by Billy's bedside while Mark took a break. My old friend was so thin and tired now. His cheeks were sunken, his dark beard giving him a hollow look. I remembered how vibrant and happy Billy and Garth had been together, how much fun we all had at concerts and picnics and outings. They'd been my staunchest allies when Jack left me, and I depended on them through thick and thin. Now Garth was gone and Billy would be gone soon, too. My parents had died years before, but I well remembered the feeling of loss and pain.

On impulse I picked up the phone book from the bedside table and thumbed through it. There it was: "William A. Manion" and an address. I dialed the number from Billy's bedside and left a brief message. "Hey, Bill. I just wanted to thank you for the coffee and the fun afternoon. You're the only W. A. Manion in the phone book, so I'm guessing this is you. I'm looking forward to our shopping trip on Saturday.

Well, thanks again." I hesitated then realized I hadn't identified myself. "Oh, damn. I should have said right away. This is Threemie. Well, duh. I suppose you guessed that! Thanks again and see you on Saturday."

I hung up the phone and smiled at Billy, whose eyes had fluttered open briefly at the sound of my voice. "Threemie?"

I smoothed back his thinning hair. "Yep. Sleep now, it's okay."

"Hmm." His eyes closed again and he relaxed against the pillow.

Mark came back a few minutes later and I left, thankful to have the visit over and guilty I was so thankful. As I walked toward the stairwell, I passed the nurses' station and saw a small, stooped man talking to one of Billy's nurses. She reminded me of my fifth grade teacher, Mrs. Shotsky: short, plump and no-nonsense. "How was Billy today?" she asked.

I shrugged. "Sleeping. I guess that's the best thing for him now."

"If he's had chemo, then yes, it is the best thing." The shrunken man smiled at me. He was a few inches taller than me but his bent posture made him seem much shorter. His pale face, trembling hands, and the haunted look in his eyes told me he was a patient, not a visitor, there.

"He's had everything," I said. "Chemo, radiation and God knows what else." I started moving away, toward the stairwell.

The stooped man moved with me, but toward the elevator, which was next to the door to the steps. "I saw you talking to an old friend of mine," he said as he pressed the Down button.

"Really? Who's that?" I pushed open the stairwell door.

"Bill Manion." The elevator dinged.

Curiosity warred with claustrophobia. Curiosity

won. "Hold the door." I scooted into the empty car behind the stooped man. "You know Bill?"

"Yep. We used to work together. Then I got laid off and lost track of him." The man touched the 'L' button. "Is that good for you?"

"What? Oh, no. Three, please. I use the catwalk." Then I remembered. I wasn't in my usual spot. The third floor was roped off. "Nope, sorry. The lobby will be fine today."

"You must not be from here." He smiled at my puzzled look. "Minnesotans say 'skyway', not 'catwalk'."

"You're right. I've been here for about ten years." The elevator descended and my stomach did an equally unpleasant plummet. "How long did you and Bill work together?" *Keep talking*, I thought. *Keep your mind off the elevator and movement and the small space and the walls and...*

"Almost twenty years. Then I got laid off and times got rough." The man's face hardened briefly, bitterness replacing the dull resignation in his tired eyes. "And I got sick."

Poor man. Losing a job was bad enough, but losing your health on top of it? I dug a business card out of my bag, my trembling fingers making the task difficult. "I work for the county and we have regular get-togethers for folks who are unemployed. Stop by sometime."

He took the card and stared at it. I recognized his skeptical look. I'd seen it often enough on the faces of job-hunters at the county employment office where I volunteered. "We call it the Coping Club," I said. "We talk about coping strategies for job hunting and dealing with unemployment. We meet on Tuesdays and Fridays."

The elevator doors opened and two people got on. I shuffled to one side to make room, restraining myself from bolting for the open door.

The man moved closer to me, speaking in a low voice. "I haven't seen Bill for a while. Have you known him long?"

"No, I just met him. We met by accident."

"Oh. Well..." He didn't look at me, his bloodshot gray eyes bouncing around the elevator car. The other two passengers were deep in conversation, ignoring us. "I suppose..."

"Yes?" *Keep talking, keep talking, keep talking.* The floor indicators were creeping past two and heading for one. After one there was the lobby. It was so close. *Keep talking.*

"I suppose since you're not from around here, you don't know about him."

"Know about him?" The door dinged and people got on. I wanted to curse them. What idiot couldn't walk down one flight of stairs? The stooped man and I were moved to the back of the car, exactly the wrong spot for me. I broke out in a light sweat and clung to the strap of my purse. "What about Bill?" I asked.

The man shook his head. "It was sad. Not a nice story."

My stomach dropped even further and I was close to clawing my way out of the space when the indicator dinged and the door finally opened. I almost fell out of the elevator, pushing past people in my haste. "What story?" I asked breathlessly in the small foyer.

The man started walking down the hall. "Rumor has it he raped someone."

Chapter 3

"I don't believe it," I said, my stomach bottoming out somewhere near my knees.

The man shrugged. "Like I said, it was a rumor."

"Was he arrested or—"

"Nah, nothing like that." We paused by the lobby desk. In the better light pouring through the windows I could tell the man wasn't much older than me, but illness had taken its toll. He had the papery, fragile look of an old man. "People talked about it down at the factory. Bill took some girl home and later there was talk that she'd been, well, messed with." The man pulled his thin winter coat tighter, bundling it up to his neck. He stuck out one hand, which I automatically took. "It was nice chatting with you. My name's Tim. I'm over here a lot." He grimaced. "Treatments, you know."

"Nice to talk to you, too," I replied absently, my brain awhirl. "I'm Mary. I hope you take me up on that offer to visit our group."

"I might. Thanks. See you around." With a little nod, he went out the revolving door, wincing as the cold north wind buffeted him.

Impossible. Absolutely impossible. Sweet,

blushing, car-restoring Bill, a rapist? My brain couldn't encompass the idea. I shook myself out of my daze and drove home, once again on autopilot. How could I verify it or not verify it? Did I dare believe it? Did I dare *not* believe it? I couldn't ask Bill about it. What could I say? "Oh, by the way, a total stranger and I chatted and he said you were a rapist. Any truth to the rumor?"

I struggled with the idea through dinner and an inane TV movie which I had no memory of watching. When the ten o'clock news came on, I was still sitting there, Major Muffin plastered against my thigh and Sgt. Snuggle propped on the cushion behind me, toying with my hair.

"...in a parking garage in Chaska, south of the metro area. For more details on this developing story, we go to Jenny Malone, on the scene."

My attention zeroed in on the TV. A petite blonde reporter was posed in front of the parking garage where I usually parked. "Paul, the police here are being very close-mouthed about the murder that occurred in this parking garage behind me. A spokeswoman for the Chaska Police Department verified the victim was an undercover officer with the Minneapolis Police Department, presumably here on police business when he was killed. We know the killing occurred on Wednesday night, around six or six-thirty. The body was discovered early on Thursday morning by party-goers who were departing from the bar across the street."

O'Grady's? Lordie, I was in that garage on Wednesday. It was probably four-thirty when I parked. That murder happened while I was eating dinner. Why didn't they find the body sooner? Weren't people coming and going in the garage? Where did it happen? Was there lots of blood?

Third floor? I remembered the crime scene tape from earlier in the day. It must all be related. I watched the perky blonde on TV as she interviewed the bartender at O'Grady's. "...never have trouble in this neighborhood. It's a nice, residential area," the solid little man said. "Most folks use that garage when they're at the hospital or to shop here. We were busy that night, of course, it being St. Pat's."

"That's what makes this crime so perplexing," the newswoman said, facing the camera again. "There were crowds of people in the garage and on the street, but no one heard anything unusual. The police are asking the public for any help they can give. If you were in the area that night, please contact the Chaska police at the number listed on your screen."

With a civic-minded sigh, I jotted the scrolling number on a notepad near my chair. "I suppose I should tell them I heard two men arguing," I told Major Muffin, who pressed against my thigh, either in sympathy or to seek warmth. "I'll think about it tomorrow and decide then." Satisfied with that compromise, I went to bed, only to toss and turn all night, dreams of Bill interspersed with memories of shouts in the parking garage.

In the cold light of morning, I was inclined to dismiss a total stranger's off-hand comment about a man I'd just met. I wasn't going to marry the guy, after all. Besides, I'd be meeting him in a public place and we'd be shopping in a public place. Surely it was okay? I could take it easy and see how it all played out. Since it was Friday, I was on Crisis Cell duty so I turned on the mobile phone the county had given me for my volunteer work. I gathered what I'd need for the day, and left the house, determined to be positive and upbeat.

I'd barely shed my coat and gotten my first cup of coffee at work before Kate cornered me. "I was going to call you last night but Martha told me I shouldn't be a mother hen. How did it go? What's he like? Did you have a good time? Are you seeing him again?"

Kate grabbed the guest chair and leaned forward anxiously. Ken loomed in the doorway, a worried frown creasing his face. "Tell us," he prompted. "How long did you talk? Was it fun? Has he been married? Is he divorced? What's he do for a living? Where does he live?"

"Good Lord, you guys!" I sat down. "Give me a break."

"Aw, c'mon," Ken urged. "We're old married people. This is a vicarious thrill. Tell all."

"He's retired, he's—"

"Ooh, he's old," Kate breathed. "That's good. You could marry him, kill him with kindness and inherit."

I shot her a dirty look. "He's not *that* old. He's fifty-six. He retired young."

"Ooh, even better," Ken whispered. "He's wealthy. What did he do—CEO? Stocks and bonds? Insider trading?"

I grinned. "A mechanic at John Deere."

Kate and Ken both leaned back, stunned. "A mechanic?" Kate asked. "Like, somebody who, like, works on engines?"

I nodded. "Exactly."

"Uh, Threemie," Ken said, "I hate to mention this, but you have a doctorate in artificial intelligence. I doubt a mechanic at John Deere has a Ph.D."

"Don't forget the Ph.D. in Social Work," I said. "I got that one after I studied fake humans. I decided I needed to study real humans first."

"Okay, two Ph.D.s and a Masters in Computer Science. I doubt he even has a B.A."

"So?"

"Not that I'm a snob or anything," Kate hastened to say, "but don't you think you'd be more comfortable with someone a bit more, well, a bit more educated?"

"Threemie's dating a mechanic?" Steven Rabinowitz, a software tester in the Pubs group, poked his head into the cube. "Can he fix my car? It's making that odd noise again."

"We're not really dating," I said, watching my cube fill up with co-workers.

Mary Jane Isaacson, customer service representative, wedged herself in next to Kate. "So what are you doing?" she asked, waggling her eyebrows. "If you're not dating."

"I'm going to help him buy a computer." I saw Marge Thornton and Barb Sandusky hover near the cube doorway, angling for a spot. "On Saturday."

"That's a date," Marge declared. "You're going out and spending money together. That counts as a date. At least it did in my day."

"A hundred years ago, yeah," Ken said, deftly dodging a slap. At sixty, Marge was the Elder States-lady of the Publications group.

"A mechanic?" Peggy Johnson asked. "A real mechanic? Like with motors?"

I nodded. "Retired."

"Retired!" Several voices shouted at once. "Lucky man!" "How old is he?" "Where does he live?" "Can he fix my car?" "Is he rich?"

I waved for quiet. "He retired after thirty years at John Deere, he restores old cars for a hobby, he's a Viet Nam vet, he has a cat, he lives in Cedar Falls, and we're going shopping together on Saturday to buy him a computer."

"A cat." Steven pounced on this information. "A match made in heaven. You have cats. And you like cars."

I rolled my eyes. "I like a car that works. Other than that, I don't care about cars. He seems like a really nice guy."

"But, Threemie..." Ken began. "The education thing—don't you think—"

Peggy, Marge, and Steven all made rude noises. "Just because Threemie collects college degrees for a hobby doesn't mean she needs to marry a rocket scientist," Peggy declared.

"I'm not marrying anyone!" I protested.

"Or do whatever with a rocket scientist," Steven said with a suggestive leer. "Is he cute? Does he have any gay friends who'd like to meet me?"

"I have no idea. Now out—all of you."

"We'll expect a complete report after your date," Ken said, nudging Marge and Steven out of his way. "Details, full and complete."

"Keep hoping," I muttered. Kate lingered behind when the others had left. "What?"

"There's something you're not telling. What is it?"

"Nothing. Well, nothing about Bill."

"Ah ha." Kate settled herself back in the guest chair and leaned conspiratorially closer. "What then? Did something happen?"

"That murder—the one on Wednesday?" Kate nodded in confirmation. "I heard some guys arguing in the parking garage. That's where I park when I go see Billy."

"Arguing? About what?"

"I don't know. It was a foreign language."

"And *you* didn't recognize it?" Kate asked skeptically. "What was it, Swahili?"

I shrugged. "I don't know if I should go to the cops or not. It was just an argument. The guy sure looked pissed off but he didn't—"

"Wait a minute, wait a minute. You *saw* the guy who was arguing?"

"I think it was him. This guy showed up in the stairwell and scared the shit out of me." I ran a hand through my hair. "Mid-fifties, round face, dark hair, big nose, brown eyes set far apart, red complexion—"

"Whoa. You should be telling the police, not me." Kate chewed on a fingernail.

"I suppose so. Do you think I'll have to look at a line-up?"

"Probably not. When were you there?"

I cheered up. "I was there earlier than they said the guy was killed."

"You should still tell the police. Maybe the guy you saw is a witness." Kate nodded as she stood up. "I think you should tell the cops. And about this Bill guy..."

I regarded her warily. "What about him?"

"Aw, heck, Threemie, we just want you to be happy. If he seems like a nice guy, who cares about the Ph.D.? Enjoy him while you can—*if* he's a nice guy." Kate shook a finger at me. "You should have him checked out. Hire a detective or something."

I almost choked. "A detective? I'm not hiring some detective. I'm going shopping with the guy, not eloping!" But a little voice in my head was saying, *not a bad idea.* No way was I going to tell her someone told me Bill might be a rapist. Kate would go ballistic. But maybe having him checked out wasn't a bad idea.

Kate glared down at me and crossed her arms over her thin chest. "Oh, all right. But you should check in with me on Saturday after your date. I want to know you're safe."

"Oh, for cryin' out loud, Kate!"

"Promise me? Report in, okay? I won't sleep until I know you're safe."

"I promise." There probably wouldn't be anything to report. Then I remembered Bill's intense dark eyes and those dimples. Not unless I got lucky.

Really lucky.

After work, I drove to the Hopkins Police Department. I wasn't sure whether to go to Chaska, where the murder occurred, or Minneapolis, where the dead cop had worked. But that would mean I'd have to drive around looking for police stations. This one in Hopkins was on my way home so it was easy. Besides, cops all talked to each other, didn't they? If I stopped here, I could make my report then go home and think about Bill. My worry about Bill was more important than being a maybe-witness to a maybe-murder.

Satisfied with my logic, I went into the modern-looking squat brick building. I talked to the desk person, who jotted information and referred me to another person, who escorted me to a harassed-looking man seated at a battered desk in a big room with other harassed-looking people.

I sat down in the offered chair and examined "Detective Marcus Sloan" if his desk nameplate was to be believed. Sloan had thick, short-cropped white/gray hair, a tanned and lined oval face with baby blue eyes and a tight, compact body in a navy sweater and jeans. Very *sharp* baby blue eyes, I decided, when he turned to me.

"You heard something on Wednesday night?" he prompted, tapping a pencil on his littered desk.

"Well, maybe," I hedged. "I was in that particular parking garage at four-thirty or so." I looked warily at the empty cup of coffee near my elbow. There was something floating on the surface of the scummy liquid and it smelled a bit rancid. I glanced around the room where people walked, stood and talked, or drank coffee. It was noisy and very beige. You'd think they could brighten it up with some paint. They should also get some nicer furniture.

"And?" Detective Sloan snapped.

Startled out of my critique of the decorating style of the Hopkins Police Department, I glared at Marcus Sloan. "No need to get shirty. I'm just doing my civic duty."

"Shirty?" He looked around the room as though requesting assistance. "That's a word?"

"It is. It means pissy." Then realizing what I said I clapped a hand over my mouth. "Oops." Was it against the law to swear at the law? I hoped not.

Sloan sat back in his chair and regarded me with those sharp blue eyes. "Why don't you just tell me what you heard?"

I decided my best bet was to speak now or forever hold my peace. "I drove through the parking garage looking for a spot. I *think* I saw two men on level three as I was looking." I frowned. "Who would've known it was St. Patrick's Day? Besides, that's such an artificial holiday." I hurried on before Sloan could comment. "I finally found a spot on the ground floor. I heard two men arguing above me. It wasn't Spanish, French, German, Dutch, Cantonese, or Arabic. I think it was an Asian dialect but I'm not sure. They were shouting. I went to the stairwell to walk up to the catwalk on level three to go to the hospital. A man came out of the stairwell at the third floor and accosted me."

Sloan's eyes widened as I recited my facts. He opened his mouth, closed it then said, "It wasn't...what did you say—Arabic or French or—"

"I'm reasonably fluent in those languages. I'd recognize them. I've never studied any of the Asian languages, except for a smattering of Cantonese. No, this was something else."

"The man 'accosted' you?" Sloan asked, leaning forward. He looked like he was struggling to suppress a grin. I could see it tugging at the corners of his mouth. His face was weathered and I saw the crinkles deepen around his eyes.

I leveled a frosty gaze at him. "Yes, he did accost me." Heavens, that sounded prim. "He appeared in the doorway as I was going to the catwalk."

"So he must have been on the fourth or fifth floor."

I considered it. "Unless he was on level three and opened the door just as I got there."

"Can you describe him? I realize you were probably nervous and the stairwell wasn't well-lighted, but—"

I shot him a pitying glance. "He was slightly taller than me, perhaps five-foot-seven. He had a heavy build, stocky and was clean-shaven except for a five o'clock shadow with a splotchy complexion and red cheeks. He had a very round face with a rather large nose." I considered Sloan's nose, which was slender. "Yes. Large nose and dark hair under a dark brown camo stocking cap. His hair looked long and curling at the back. Hmm. It might have some gray," I amended. "Dark eyebrows and dark eyes." I looked at Sloan's baby blues. "Brown, I believe, or perhaps hazel. He had a slight scar near one eyebrow, rather Harry Potter-ish. He was wearing brown pants, a dark blue jacket with some kind of sports insignia here." I gestured vaguely to my right breast. Sloan's eyes followed the movement then returned to my face. "He was probably in his early to mid-fifties, quite athletic looking, and very fit." I sat back. "That's all I remember. But of course, I was nervous." I smiled. "And it was dark."

Sloan's jaw hinged back up with an audible snap. "This was at four-thirty?"

I nodded. "Possibly later. It probably has nothing to do with the murder."

"Maybe. We're not exactly sure down to the minute."

"I thought the Chaska police were handling it. Or was that the royal 'we'?"

Sloan sighed and leaned back in his chair, lacing his fingers over his flat stomach. "Okay. So I was shirty. We didn't expect a witness."

"I'm hardly a witness," I pointed out. "I simply heard two men arguing."

"In some language other than French, Spanish, Arabic or—" Sloan's voice trailed away as he regarded me. "We'd better put you with a sketch artist and see what we get." He stood up.

I remained seated. "Now?"

He nodded. "We'll go to Minneapolis. Technically it's their case since it was their cop who was shot."

"I thought you were all one big happy cop family."

"We are. Is there a problem with going to Minneapolis?" he asked, staring down at me.

"Your manners are a bit abrupt." I got to my feet. "Perhaps I have plans tonight. Perhaps I'm busy. Perhaps I don't want to go to Minneapolis."

He snagged his jacket from his chair. "Perhaps you'll want to do your civic duty." He started walking out of the room.

"Perhaps I already did my duty by coming here. Is this necessary? The timing's wrong and why would a police officer be speaking in some foreign language? I don't even know if the man who surprised me was one of the men who were arguing. Why would—"

"The undercover agent was Laotian," Sloan said as he steered me out of the police station and to the parking lot. "That hasn't been on the news."

"Laotian," I murmured. That would fit. The language had sounded vaguely Asian and there was a large Hmong population in the Twin Cities. "That might make sense," I conceded as Sloan led me to a large dark sedan. "But the man I saw was Caucasian. Of course, that doesn't mean he couldn't speak Laotian but—" I stopped, suddenly aware I was about to get into an unmarked police car. "Do we have to do this?"

Sloan opened the back door of the car for me.

"Yep."

"Aw, shit," I whispered as the door closed. I peered into the front at the various radios, switches, and knobs on the dashboard. Unlike a squad car, this one didn't have a grate separating me from the front. I was just leaning forward to examine the equipment when Sloan slid into the driver's seat.

He gave me a quelling look. "No touching."

I glared at him. What a spoilsport. "Can we drive with a siren on?"

"No."

Mega-spoilsport. "How about—"

"No." He started the car and pulled out of the parking lot.

"Aren't you cheerless?" I stared out the window. "I'm just doing my duty and I'd think you'd like to accommodate me." I slid a sidelong glance his way. He was fiddling with the radio, speaking into a handheld microphone. I tried to eavesdrop, but he had low-voiced conversation down to an art form. "You shouldn't talk and drive at the same time. I think it's against the law."

After a long conversation, he hung up the radio and flicked a glance my way. "Did you have plans tonight?"

"I have to be somewhere at seven-thirty," I said haughtily. I had the Coping Club tonight, which lasted from seven-thirty until nine. I also wanted plenty of time to think about Bill, plan what to wear and what to say and...hmm. He mentioned dinner. Would I need to dress up? I looked down at my battered snow sneakers and mentally ran through my closet choices. No, dress-up was out. I'd need to send him email and...oh, shit, that's right, he didn't have email at home. Maybe jeans and...

"I'll try to make it quick," Sloan said, steering us onto the busy interstate. "You're the only person who's come forward and said they were in that garage that night."

*Well, aren't I an idiot? I could've just gone on my merry way and no one would be the wiser.* "I'm afflicted by a conscience," I muttered, glaring out my window. "It comes of all those years protesting the Viet Nam war and trying to get Nixon impeached. Maybe everyone else was too drunk to remember being in the garage. It *was* St. Pat's Day, after all."

"Yeah, we thought of that. So, what do you do for a living? It said on the intake form that you write computer documentation?" He glanced at me then back at the traffic, merging and changing lanes with effortless ease. I was secretly impressed. I detested rush hour traffic and admired anyone who could negotiate it without road rage.

"I assist in the design of new computer chips. I document the engineering specs as we map out the chips. It's like an audit trail of ideas." There was a long pause. I glanced at Sloan, who was staring ahead stoically. I recognized that look and sighed. "It's a bit arcane."

He nodded. "Uh-hunh." He got off the freeway and began to take a series of side streets, making left and right turns with surprising frequency.

I looked around. I seldom went into downtown Minneapolis and when I did, I stuck to simple routes that were easy to remember. "Where are we?"

"South of the city on Lyndale. It's easier than the freeway at this time of day."

I returned to studying the houses flashing by my window. "How was the policeman killed? Was it icky?" I caught a glimpse of Sloan's wide grin then it vanished. "You know what I mean—was it bloody or nasty? I didn't see any blood."

The light from oncoming headlights illuminated Sloan's craggy face. "Not a lot of blood and he was hidden near the front of the car. It was hard to see."

"Well, I still don't understand why—"

"Here we are."

"We're where?" Sloan crossed the intersection, took another left and suddenly a large white building loomed ahead of us. "Is that the jail?"

He parked the car. "It's the Administration Center. The jail's next door. The sketch artist is here." He got out as I fumbled with my door, which apparently had no door handles on the inside. Sloan came around to my side and opened it. "I just wanted you to know I've only told a couple of people you've come forward as a witness." He held the door for me.

"I'm not really a witness. I just heard some men."

"Look," Sloan said, slamming the door and leaning one hand on it, effectively cutting off my escape route. "I'm going to be straight with you. We don't want it advertised there's a witness. We're trying to keep as much as possible out of the media. So I'd appreciate it if you wouldn't tell your boyfriend or your friends about all of this."

"Was it drugs?"

Sloan frowned. "Something like that."

"What do you mean, *something like that*? It's either drugs or it's not. Why do you presume I have a boyfriend, as you so quaintly phrased it?"

He grinned. "Okay—'gentleman friend'. Does that sound better?"

I settled my purse more firmly on my shoulder. "I can keep a secret. Lead on and let's get this over with."

"Oh, c'mon." He led me to a back door labeled *Official Entrance*. "Isn't this fun?"

"Right up there with root canals and the flu. If I can't allude to secrets and dumbfound my friends then it's not much use, is it?"

"Dumbfound?" He swiped a card through a card reader then opened the door for me. "Allude? Accost?

Where do you get those words? I've never heard anybody use them in conversation."

"It's your native tongue. You should learn to use it." I preceded him into a long hallway. I looked around then moved off at a brisk pace in what appeared to be the correct direction. "There are approximately one hundred thousand words in use at any time in the English Language and that's not counting the slang. Most people only use a tenth of those words. You should stretch a bit."

"I'll remember that." Sloan brushed past me and led the way down the hall, past several corridors, into a main hallway and a tall desk. He pulled out a wallet, showed it to the officer on duty, signed some forms then led me to a bank of elevators. My steps lagged when I saw where he was heading. "What?" he asked, slowing his pace to match mine.

"I don't like elevators. I got stuck in one once."

Sloan looked from the banks of elevators to me. "It's on the twentieth floor. We'll take the express. We'll be there before you know it."

I followed him, wedging myself into the corner of the elevator. Other people packed in around us. Sloan leaned against the wall, looking at me. "How long were you stuck?"

I huddled into the corner of the elevator and stared up into his blue eyes. "Five hours. I don't like little places." I started to look around, but he said,

"Look at me. It's okay. These elevators never break down. Where did that happen? Was it here in town? I don't remember hearing about it."

"I was in California at a conference. There was an earthquake and the elevators stopped."

Sloan's eyes widened. "An earthquake? Really?"

"It was just a tiny one. That's what everybody said. But the elevators stop when there's an earthquake. It was in the hotel. There were four of us stuck between floors. They finally pried the doors open and we had to crawl out."

Sloan leaned nearer to me. I gulped when the car stopped and the doors opened. "That's the tenth floor. We're almost there." He stared at me and I stared back, mesmerized. "It must be hard to deal with. Elevators are everywhere. Is that why you took the stairs at the garage?"

The floor surged under me. I swallowed the nausea that threatened and tried to focus on Detective Sloan's eyes but all I could remember was crawling out of the elevator years ago. I'd been so afraid it would lurch and cut me in half.

"Was it?" he asked insistently.

"Was what?"

There was a dinging noise and Sloan straightened up. "We're here." He moved ahead of me, forging a path through the crowded elevator. I followed, the open space beckoning to me beyond the gaping doors. As my purse banged someone, I turned to apologize.

The round-faced man was staring at me.

Chapter 4

"Holy shit." I gaped at the man as the elevator doors closed.

Sloan was already striding down the hall, talking over his shoulder at me. "Do you want some water or something? You looked white as a sheet there for a minute."

"That was him," I stammered.

"That was who?"

"Him. The man. He was there."

Sloan stopped and looked back at me. "Where?"

"There!" I gestured toward the elevator. "There. He was there."

"Okay, wait a minute. The guy was on the elevator?" Sloan demanded. "The guy who didn't speak French or Spanish or whatever?" I nodded, too nauseous and frightened to speak. "Ah, shit." He looked around. "Okay. You sit there. Wait for me." He gestured to a bank of chairs outside a door signed with *Forensic Pathology: Intake.*

I sank into the chair, clutching my purse. Sloan hurried off down the hall, pulling out a cell phone and talking into it. "I'm going to have a policewoman come here. Don't move!" he called back over his shoulder.

I dabbed at my forehead and nodded acknowledgement. I watched people going in and out of the office next to me, often carrying large containers of unsavory looking things or items that looked suspiciously like weapons. They were probably murder weapons, I decided. What else might be going into a Pathology lab?

I didn't want to think about it. I pulled out Paula Palm Pilot and accessed my email to divert my attention from the grisly goings-on next to me. I had one from Steven, reminding me to 'ask my new boyfriend about car repair.' Yeah, right. I also had one from Bill.

*I wanted to make dinner reservations for us tomorrow; is there a restaurant you'd prefer? Please call me if there is one. I bought computer furniture today and I'll be home tonight putting it together. I'm looking forward to seeing you at noon.*

He'd included his mobile and home phone number and had signed the message with "WAM". I smiled when I saw that. I stared at the wall opposite me, trying to reconcile the man who'd sent that email with a possible rapist. I decided to call him after Coping Club. I couldn't think of any way to work the conversation around to possible felonies in his past.

It just didn't add up.

Twenty minutes later Sloan reappeared, looking even more harassed than before. "Where's that policewoman?" he snarled, striding down the hall.

"He got away?"

"Someone was supposed to meet you." Sloan looked around the hallway, scowling. "Hell, you were supposed to have protection."

"Your comforting manner isn't working," I pointed out. "You need to improve that."

Sloan's attention snapped to me and he nodded,

smiling slowly. "Yeah. I know. Come on." He led the way down the hall again. "We need that picture."

"This hasn't been a pleasant experience," I mentioned as Sloan hurried down the hall, to another hall and through a corridor to another hallway. "This was supposed to be just a quick stop at the Hopkins Police Department then I was going to go on my merry way." We came to an unmarked door and Sloan opened it. "There were people walking into that office back there carrying body parts."

"How do you know they were body parts?" Sloan looked around the room and steered me to a chair near a table where a computer sat.

"I watch TV. I know body parts when I see them." I sank wearily into the chair, which was far more comfortable than the one I'd occupied a few minutes previously. My stomach rumbled. "Sorry. I didn't have much lunch."

He looked chagrined. "I'm buying when this is over. You pick the place."

I wrinkled my nose. "As long as I can erase the memory of those body parts. So why was that man on the elevator? I thought only police were in this building?"

Sloan nodded glumly. "Yeah." He looked up as a young man entered the room to take a seat at the computer across the desk from me. "That's the problem."

I considered his words then his meaning sank in. "Oh."

Sloan nodded. "Yeah." He smiled wryly. "Oh."

****

I spent an interesting half-hour describing the round-faced man while Sloan watched and the young police artist dabbled on the computer, finally composing a picture that looked somewhat like the man I'd seen.

Sloan's offer of a meal apparently extended only to places in Hopkins. "Sorry," he said as we drove back to the police department where my car was parked. "I'm on duty and I've got some work to get caught up on."

"No problem," I said magnanimously. "Just drive through Wendy's and I'll grab a salad."

"I can spring for something better than fast food."

"I'm on a diet. Anyplace else would be wasted."

He eyed me in the rear view mirror. "Diet? Why?" I was flattered and flustered and I guess it must have showed because he grinned at me.

"Thank you. I have five pounds to go before I'm back to where I want to be."

"I don't know what it is with women, it seems like they're always dieting." He pulled into the drive-through lane and shouted my order into the remote system. If the teenaged clerk was surprised to see a woman being chauffeured in an unmarked Crown Vic, he didn't show it.

Sloan pulled into the parking lot at the police station and I directed him to my car. As I got out, clutching my salad sack, I decided to broach the question that had been bugging me all night. "So, listen. You're a cop."

"Yeah?" He leaned against the Crown Vic warily and regarded me, arms crossed on his chest. "So?"

"I have a question maybe you can answer." I swung my sack idly, wondering how to phrase it.

"I'll give it a shot." He gave me an encouraging nod, his hair gleaming bright white in the light from the parking lights.

"Let's say you meet somebody. You think he's a nice guy and you're kind of going out on a date with him."

He grinned at me. "Not quite my cup of tea, but I think I see where this is going."

I swung my sack. "Rhetorically speaking, of course. But then you meet somebody else who says that person might not be as nice as you think. So...what do you do?"

He stared at me impassively for a long minute. "Who's this other person who's dishing the dirt on the guy?"

I shrugged. "Just somebody I met."

"How well do you know the guy? The guy you're going to sort of date?"

"Not well at all. That's the problem. We met by accident and..." I didn't know how to tell a police stranger I was infatuated with a man I barely knew, a man who had kissed me in the parking garage and for whom I would have willingly torn off my clothes.

"Go with your gut," Sloan said decisively. "Oh, you could hire a P.I. and investigate the guy, but that will just give you some facts. You need to go with your instincts. Do they tell you he's an okay guy?"

I nodded.

"Then give it a try. Just be smart about it. Don't go anywhere alone with the guy, make sure you check in with somebody—you know the drill?"

I nodded again, glad I was getting confirmation of what I thought was right. I clicked Stella's remote and the interior car lights came on.

"Miss Madison?"

I looked at Sloan as I stowed the salad bag on Stella's passenger seat.

"Be careful. If you have any hesitations about this guy, just call me." He handed me a business card, which I stuffed into my coat pocket.

"Thanks. I will." I smiled apologetically. "It's weird being in the dating game at my age."

He laughed softly. "Join the group. I know the feeling. Thanks for helping tonight. I'll call you if anything comes up."

"Thanks." I got into Stella and drove off, glancing once in the rear view mirror to see him watching me. Then he was lost to sight as I turned the corner and got onto Main Street, which led to the workforce center and my waiting Coping Club members.

Volunteering has always been a part of my life, starting in hospitals during my teens and continuing through my first college degree in artificial intelligence. It was while trying to mimic human thinking I realized how little I knew about real humans, so I went to school to get a formal degree in sociology. When I moved to Minnesota after my divorce I continued a tradition I'd started in Pittsburgh where I'd been living and formed a Coping Club at the county employment office.

A co-worker and I took turns running the session and also manning the Crisis Cell. We each carried a special cell phone with a phone number dedicated to a crisis line for people who were coping with unemployment and the miseries that went along with it. Hal Burns and I alternated days when we were on call.

I gulped down my salad in the break room at the County Employment Center surrounded by vending machines and other volunteers then entered Conference Room B. All three board rooms were occupied on Friday nights with different employment strategy sessions, staffed by volunteers like me. The regular staff was all burned out after a week of dealing with the public.

I greeted the regulars and noted three new faces, one of which was Tim from the hospital. I was pleased to see him, not only to offer him help but to have a chance to pump him for information about Bill. I handed out the Crisis Cell phone number to the newbies and gave them my usual explanation.

"Hal Burns and I take turns manning the phone,

so if you don't like me, don't call on Friday, Sunday, or Tuesday, that's when I'm on phone duty." I always smiled when I said this because I wanted folks to know I really didn't care if they preferred Hal to me. I moved my hair away from my right ear so they could see the phone receiver. "It's always on whenever one of us is on call and someone will always answer. So don't be afraid to use it, that's why we hand out the number." I looked around the table. "This is a free form session, so if anybody has something to start with, let's get going."

That little bit of encouragement was all it took and we were off and running. The Coping Club was part bitch session, part sympathy party, and part constructive job-hunting strategies. During a break in the action, I turned to Tim, who'd been listening to everyone with polite interest. "What's your story, Tim? What happened that brought you here tonight?"

He stared at the faux wood tabletop then smiled bitterly. He'd probably been handsome once, but his illness robbed him of that. His brown hair was thinning, his skin was an unhealthy gray color, and his clothes hung on him. My father fought cancer and I recognized its effects.

"Three years ago I was on top of the world," he said in a low, rough voice. "I had a great job, a great wife, and a great life. I had seven years to go to retirement then I could coast. It would be Easy Street for the rest of my life."

"Oh, man, I've heard this before," George muttered. I shot him a quelling look and he shrugged. George was a regular Club attendee and he knew our rules: everybody was allowed their grievance and a chance to air it.

"Three years ago I got laid off and now look." Tim wiped at his nose with a grimy handkerchief and swallowed hard. I could tell he was fighting grief. "My wife left me, my kids moved away, and my old life—the house, the camper, the SUV, the car, the weekends at the lake—they're all gone, either sucked away in the divorce or eaten up by hospital bills. Only my pension is left, but I can't touch it for another four years." He coughed, a rasping, hacking sound that made me wince. When he finished, he was trembling. "At least the pension will give survivor benefits to the kids."

A murmur of sympathy echoed around the table. I leaned forward. "Have you had any luck job hunting?"

"I'm too sick," he mumbled. "Besides, nobody wants anybody my age. I'd need retraining and nobody wants to waste money on somebody's who's sick and older."

I started to point out that was age discrimination but Doris, another regular, said, "No way to prove that, either." Heads nodded agreement.

She was right. Age or health discrimination was hard to prove and hard to prosecute. "There are retraining programs," I suggested.

"I've been a mechanic all my life," he said flatly. "It's what I do."

"Maybe we can find something related to that. Maybe—"

He huddled into his bulky sweater, almost visibly shivering. I recognized that hunched, agonized posture. When my father was sick even on a mild night, he'd be freezing.

The spasm of shivering ignited something in Tim's chest and he coughed again, hiding his face with the handkerchief then leaning back, exhausted, when it finished.

"Have you ever thought about doing something to the son of a bitch who fired you?" George asked.

Tim's bloodshot eyes zeroed in on George. While I may have disliked the subject, I was grateful

George diverted Tim's attention. "Sure," he rasped. "He's healthy and happy and going on with his life like nothing happened. Believe me, if I could figure out a way to hurt him, I would. I've got nothing to lose."

How could I combat anger and depression like that? Anything I thought about saying would sound either trite or condescending.

George bailed me out again. "You've got something to lose," he said. "You've got your dignity. Your pride."

Tim's mouth twisted in a parody of a smile. "I don't have much of that left. The damn drugs have taken it all away." His eyes went to the window and I followed his gaze. Snow was falling, reflected in the parking lot lights. "I remember cross-country skiing once with Darlene and the kids. We rented skis at the park and went out for the afternoon. I used to love wintertime." His hand clenched on the table. "Now I can't wait for spring. I can't wait to be warm again." His gaze returned to me and he smiled apologetically. "Sorry to be such a downer."

"That's why we're here, man," Carlos said. "You need to unload, you come to us. Or to Mama Madison." He grinned at me. "I've called the Crisis Cell and cried on her shoulder."

"I know you don't want to hear this, but it's more constructive to put your anger to good use," I said. "The person who fired you was probably told to do it by someone higher up on the food chain. For all you know, maybe he was laid off, too, after you."

Tim shook his head adamantly. "I stay in touch with the old gang. Most of the old guys like me are retired, and they're replacing 'em with machines or younger guys. It sucks, but there you are. There are no old mechanics. It's hard on the legs and the hands."

I hadn't thought about that. Bill's hands were

rough and callused, and a bit knobby, maybe from arthritis? I could only imagine the back problems a mechanic might have from bending over all the time, peering into the innards of an engine. "But maybe there's something related to your field," I insisted. "Like teaching or—"

He coughed again, shaking his head the whole time. "Nah. That's okay. I've got some disability and still have the health insurance, so I'm getting by," he finally wheezed. He shot me an obviously insincere smile. "I'm getting by."

Carlos took up the conversational gauntlet, complaining about the computerization of his old job on the assembly line. We passed the remainder of the session discussing retraining options. I just tossed out ideas, knowing none were viable but also knowing hope was a powerful palliative for these dispossessed people.

When the group broke up, Tim lingered behind to talk with me. "I appreciate what you said and I don't want you to think I haven't looked for a job. I did look a lot but then I got sick and Darlene left me and..." He shrugged, bony shoulders lifting and falling in his worn coat.

His defeatist attitude was annoying, but I was accustomed to that. It was easy for people who were unemployed to take on a 'the world hates me' attitude, especially when they went to interview after interview and were constantly rejected.

"How long has it been since you were laid off?" I put on my coat and slung my bag over my shoulder. "It must seem like a lot of things are ganging up against you. After a while, you start to dread job hunting because you're afraid of getting yet another brush-off."

Tim kept pace with me as we left the room. "Yeah, and it's tough now, too. I was used to sharing with somebody, but my wife left me when times got bad."

He was probably better off without her, but I didn't express that opinion. Maybe there was more to the mysterious Darlene's vanishing than met the eye. Who knew? There were as many reasons for divorce as there were people in the world, but it all boiled down to one: sometimes you just don't get along anymore. It was a depressing thought added to my already hectic day. "You said you're in touch with the people you worked with. Maybe you could contact them and see if they have any job leads?"

A brisk wind greeted us as we emerged from the building. The snow was swirling, more nuisance than accumulation.

Tim shivered and tucked himself, turtle-like, into his coat, wrapping a long length of scarf several times around his throat. "I see some of them down at Benteen's. That's a bar in Chaska where I go sometimes." He glanced at me, his face almost obscured by the faded brown and beige scarf. "That's where Bill—you know, where he picked up that girl folks said he messed with."

"Really?" I tried to sound disinterested, but a small sliver of annoyance was starting to prickle me. This kind of rumor was so hard to prove or disprove. I think my anger must have shown in my voice because Tim's eyes narrowed when I said, "If there weren't any charges filed, then maybe it's all just a story the girl made up."

"I suppose she figured there was no good reporting him to the police since he's friends with the cops in town. He's lived there all his life. Hell, he probably went to school with some of the police." Tim's disgust at this evidence of upright citizenry was clear in his voice.

"Nothing wrong with that," I snapped, clicking on Stella's lights with the remote. "In today's world, a woman can accuse a man of just about anything and someone will listen to her. I wonder why this girl didn't do anything."

Tim paused by my car door, shoulders hunched. "He was a floor boss at the factory. Maybe she was afraid she'd lose her job."

Oh, shit. Bill was her boss? This was worse than I'd thought. I took my disappointment out on poor Tim. "If it was a union shop, and I'll guess it was, there probably wasn't much danger of that. It sounds like she just didn't want to take responsibility for her own actions. That happens a lot nowadays."

He backed away. "I suppose you think that about me. I suppose you figure I'm just whining about not working and I didn't do anything to find a job."

"I didn't say that but it is a trap that people can fall into. It's a lot easier to blame the world for our problems than it is to look at how we might solve them." Good God, I sounded like a priss again. First Detective Sloan and now this poor man—since when had I become such a righteous bitch? "I'm sorry, but—"

"You'll see what I mean," he snapped. "If you go out with Bill Manion, you'll find out what he's like. I tried to warn you. He's playing with you, like he did with CiCi. Did you ask him? He used her then he walked away. Bill told people she was a slut. He ruined her reputation."

"Now wait a minute," I said, tossing my purse into Stella and turning to confront him. "You can't go around saying things like that. Bill isn't here to defend himself. You're just spreading rumors if you do something like that."

"You ask him about it. Ask him about what happened with CiCi down at Benteen's. Be careful, though. He's rough and he'll hurt you—not just break your heart, but he'll hurt you. Ask any woman he's slept with, they'll tell you. He likes it rough."

With a sad shake of his head, Tim stalked away, leaving me shivering in the cold snow that was falling.

## Chapter 5

I hate confrontation of any kind. My usual reaction is to flee, and I stayed true to form on this night. I got into Stella, fumbled the key into the ignition, and tore out of the parking lot as though the demons of hell were after me.

I suppose, in a way, they were. Why couldn't life be simple? Why did I have to be an almost-witness to a murder? Why did I have to be alone? Why did Jack divorce me? Why couldn't I trust Bill?

Why the hell was all this crap happening to me?

My street was quiet when I pulled into the driveway. I thought about what Sloan said as I fed the felines and settled down with a glass of wine to calm my nerves. He was right. A total stranger told me something nasty about Bill, but it was Bill I'd talked to, Bill I'd spent two hours with. I had to trust my instincts on this.

But I also had to reconfirm my instincts. I dug my Palm out of my bag and checked the email message Bill sent me. I called the home number listed.

"Damn," he said when he picked up.

"Hello?"

"I'm sorry. I dropped my screwdriver and Magoo is batting around a part I need for this bookcase I'm putting together. I bought a bunch of computer furniture today so we'd have some place to put my new computer tomorrow."

I laughed. "Magoo?"

"My cat. Is this Mary? I mean, Threemie?"

"Yepper. How'd you guess?"

"I was hoping it was you. Otherwise I'd have to go someplace and check my email." He laughed and I could imagine his dark eyes crinkling with amusement. "So how was your day?"

"It was odd. I'll tell you about it sometime."

"I had a weird day, too. The bank called and said somebody tried to use my credit card."

"What?"

"Yeah. Somebody tried to pull that identity fraud thing. I think I know how it happened, too. It was last night at the library."

I sipped my wine, tension easing out of me at the sound of his casual voice. It felt natural to sit there, talk with him, and have him share details of his version of a hectic day. I could easily imagine him plopped down in a chair, long legs stretched out and relaxed as he watched the falling snow, too. "What happened at the library?"

"I had to prove who I was to the librarian when I asked to use a terminal. I pulled out my wallet and ID and I'll bet I dropped a receipt."

"But most receipts don't have credit card numbers on them any more."

"This was from the hardware store downtown. Charlie hasn't gotten around to electronic card readers yet. He still has the kind that makes the carbon copy. I bought some flower seeds and some fertilizer. Hey, maybe you can help me, you're the gardener. I need to find some nice flowers for the front of my house. But I guess I shouldn't ask you to help me with that, too. You're already helping me with the computer thing."

"Oh, I'm sure there's something you can help me with, to pay me back," I said idly, swinging my bunny slipper off one foot.

"You just name it."

I waggled my eyebrows at the TV set, silent and dark. Just the sound of Bill's voice was getting me hot and bothered. Oh, yeah. He could help me.

Then I remembered Tim's scowling face and my bunny paused on my foot. Who to believe? Damn. "I may take you up on that. How did the bank handle it?"

"They put a stop on my credit card and I have a pre-approved amount for the weekend. I'll get a new card next week and my banker will keep an eye out for anything suspicious. Would you mind stopping by the bank in the morning before we go shopping? I want to make sure it's all in place."

"No problem. You're lucky to have such a pro-active banker."

"That's one of the benefits of living in a small town."

I remembered Tim's assertion that Bill's status in a small town allowed him to get away with...what? "I've never lived in a small town. I suppose everybody knows your business, hmm? That's what I've heard."

"Oh, sure. And since I've lived here all my life, I've got friends I grew up with who are still here and friends of my family. That can work for and against you, of course. Magoo, give me that." I heard the sound of a scuffle then Bill came back on the line. "That cat just loves anything crinkly. He was dragging away the sack. Listen, about dinner tomorrow night..."

"Would it be okay if we don't go anyplace fancy to eat?" I hurried on. "I'm not much for dressing up. I thought maybe we could sort of hang out, go to a bar or something."

I could almost hear him sigh with relief. "That'd be great. I'm not a gourmet guy. I'm more burgers and fries."

"I'm more wine-in-a-box than a cork."

"Really?"

"Really." I lay back and put my feet up on the couch back, sharing the space with Sgt. Snuggle. "Tell me some other things that you like besides burgers and fries. What about favorite books or magazines?" I wiggled my bunny slippers, watching the light snow falling outside.

"Well..."

"What? You can tell me—*Playboy*? *Penthouse*?"

He laughed out loud. "No, nothing like that. It's just that...well, you've got a college degree so you'll think this is dumb but...I'm working on a Bachelor's Degree from the University. I've only got ten classes to go. I've been doing one or two a year. I started taking classes at the Community College and now I'm finishing at the University."

"Really? In what?"

"Mechanical engineering."

"Wow. That's a tough one. So what classes do you have left?"

"I've been mixing up the liberal arts with the engineering. This semester I'm taking philosophy. I'm reading Kant right now."

I almost choked on my wine. "You're kidding."

"Nope."

"I didn't think anybody read Kant. I thought people read the Cliff Notes of Kant. I'm impressed."

"So what are you reading now?"

I looked at the steamy romance novel sitting on the arm of the couch. "Fiction." I sipped some more then blurted, "Hey, Bill?"

"Hmm?"

"How come it's so easy to talk to you?" I stared out the window, suddenly mortified at what I was saying. "I mean, I'm usually such a klutz around guys. But I'm really relaxed with you." Oh well. I guess I was still a klutz.

"I'm the same way. It's hard to meet people. And I'm too shy to try those dating services."

I almost choked again. "You, shy? Mr. 'Grab a girl and kiss her'?" I laughed. "And that email you sent me? Honestly, Bill, that wasn't shy at all!"

"Oh, well, email. That's easy. It's tough when you're looking at somebody and saying those things." There was a long pause. "But it's not tough with you."

"I know." I stared at the snow, wishing he were sitting with me on the couch. Wishing he was lying with me on the couch. Wishing he was lying with me with very little clothes on. "Well, I'd better go. I'm looking forward to tomorrow."

"I am, too. Threemie?"

"Hmm?"

"Good night."

"Good night." I hung up the phone, staring out into the night.

Sloan was right. I had to go with my gut.

Bill Manion was a good guy.

\*\*\*\*

At nine o'clock on Saturday morning I turned off the Crisis Cell, mentally turning the reins over to Hal for his shift. Then I worked on the thing that worried me since I woke up: I agonized over my clothing choices, supervised by Major Muffin. I held up sweater after sweater, regarding myself critically in the mirror. "No. It's too dark" or "I'd have to wear those black pants" or "It's too tight, isn't it?" or "It's too loose." The Muffin Man yawned as I finally pulled out a pastel-shaded sweater in a patchwork pattern. "This one." Muffin started to bathe. "Right.

This is the one."

I pulled on the sweater, jeans, and sneakers then went to the bathroom to dab on my meager makeup, the conundrum of Bill occupying my thoughts. What did Tim mean when he said Bill was 'rough'? Good heavens, if he'd abused someone he probably would have been arrested. Should I ask Sloan to look into it? Then I remembered Kate's assertion that I should hire someone to investigate Bill. Was she right? Why wasn't Bill married? Of course, he was shy in a lot of ways. I remembered the feeling of Bill's chest under my hand. I hope he wasn't *too* shy. It would be nice to have a man who'd like to...

Oh, shit. I stared at myself in the mirror. Did I need to get condoms? What if this led to something? What if he wanted to—? I gulped. It was years since I had sex. Birth control wasn't an issue; a hysterectomy years before had solved that dilemma but what about, well, disease or—I thought of Billy and Garth. Oh, God. I needed to buy some condoms.

I had no idea what to buy. I patted on blusher, dabbed mascara and ran fingers through my shaggy hair. There were probably a million varieties. How hard could it be? I grinned. No pun intended. I would stop at Walgreen's. Maybe buy some aspirin with it as camouflage. It paid to be prepared.

I thought about my Dating Dilemma all the way to Chaska, where I was to meet Bill. I could probably call Sloan and ask him to check up on Bill, but that seemed so...untrusting. Maybe I should have him check on Tim? That idea occupied my thoughts for almost the entire twelve-mile trip from my house to the parking garage. It seemed like Tim was anxious to bad-mouth Bill, but why? From the way it sounded, they may have worked together but Bill retired a year or more after Tim was laid off. I wasn't exactly sure of the dates, though. Was Tim just being civic-minded and trying to warn me away from potential danger? Or was something else at play? I was sure he wasn't interested in me in a male-female way. He didn't act like it and besides, he was too sick. Romance wasn't on his radar screen.

On the other hand, Tim had no reason to steer me wrong. I just met the guy. The thought nagged me during the short drive, bothered me as I parked, locked Stella, and hurried out of the parking garage. Bill was waiting outside the Kindest Bean, walking forward to meet me with a big smile. I looked up and saw his clear, honest expression.

It had to be bullshit. He seemed like such a nice guy. It felt natural to walk up to him and kiss him lightly on the lips. "Hello, there." I looked up into his dark, navy blue eyes, my hands on his shoulders holding me steady.

He smiled, dimples flashing. "I'm always worried you won't show up. I keep thinking I must be dreaming you. We talk at night and in the morning I'm afraid you won't be there."

I took his arm. "I'm here and ready to spend your money."

"Bank first, then spending." He led me to a dark green pickup truck parked on the street, helping me into the passenger side before going to the driver's side and getting in. "I'm glad you don't mind stopping by the bank. It's on our way out of town anyway."

"Not a problem. You need to make sure that kind of thing is taken care of." The truck was immaculately clean inside and out. I thought guiltily of Stella, encrusted with snow-spray and with a few candy wrappers drifting around the interior. I made a mental note to head to the car wash as soon as I could.

I looked around as we drove through the small town. Billy's hospital was on the outskirts and I never had any need to go beyond the hospital environs. "Have you always lived here?"

"Yep. My folks used to farm outside of town. After I got back from 'Nam, I got a job at the factory and an apartment in town. I kept thinking I'd travel, maybe explore the world but somehow I just stayed put." He glanced at me. "I suppose I'm boring that way."

"Not boring. Just settled. I've lived a lot of different places and never really settled until I came here. I like Minnesota. It suits me."

"I'm glad you like it, too." He smiled at me as we pulled into an open municipal parking lot behind several three-story brick buildings. "Here we are. This shouldn't take long." He came around the truck and caught me as I was scrambling down. "I guess I need to get a step for you."

I grinned. "I'm an old hand at maneuvering in tall spaces."

He led the way to the back door of the bank, opening it for me and letting me precede him. The bank was charming, a throwback to an older style of building with tall windows letting the light stream in, floral carpet and a wooden island where people could fill out their financial forms. It reminded me of Jimmy Stewart's Building and Loan from *It's a Wonderful Life*.

The bank stop was shaping up to be like a scene from that movie. A young woman greeted Bill when we entered and was introduced to me as Sada Jenkins, the clerk who'd assisted Bill initially on the previous day. While not exactly flirtatious, I could tell she was interested in Bill by the way she moved, the way she stood close to him, and the way she gave me a quick, dismissive glance.

"It's a good thing we caught that attempted fraud so quickly," she said, leading Bill and me toward a row of offices that flanked the wall opposite the teller windows. "We haven't had many cases like it here, but it's becoming such an epidemic in the city."

Before we could enter one of the four offices, a tall, balding man with a paunch left an office we'd passed and gestured to us. "I've got your copies right here, Bill." He smiled at Sada. "I wanted to take care of it myself. Come on in and sit down."

"Thanks, Emil, you didn't have to do that." Bill went into the office and I followed, glancing back at Miss Jenkins, who was shooting the paunchy man a look of pure animosity. I almost laughed out loud. I'm sure she'd been looking forward to being Bill's Knight in Shining Armor and she didn't appreciate having her role usurped.

"Hey, I may be the bank manager, but I'm also your old quarterback. I still like to take care of my teammates." He smiled at me and stuck out a hand. "Emil Swenson."

"Mary Madison." I shook his hand and sat down in the offered chair. "So you and Bill went to school together?"

"Yep. Bill played tight end and I was quarterback." He smiled as he pulled out a manila folder from the desk drawer. "We won the state championships."

Tight end? I smiled at the wicked thought that crossed my mind.

"I can't figure this," Bill said as he settled into the chair next to me. "Why would anyone pull this on me? I don't have that much money to steal."

Emil smiled. "Doesn't matter why. It happens all the time. But this loan application..." He tapped the folder. "The stuff that's missing is important but not critical—years at your current address, previous address. At least they didn't have the right social security number. We have your number on file from when you opened your account with us." He grinned at Bill, his cherubic face flushed and pink. "That was about forty years ago, wasn't it?"

"Not that long." Bill glanced at me then smiled. "Yeah, maybe it was, now that I think about it. I got my account here when I opened a paper route. So did you contact the police?"

Emil nodded. "We also put a freeze on your checking, savings, and credit cards, just to be on the safe side. I put a call into the credit card company and we set a limit for this weekend. Anything over that and it'll be rejected by the system." He slid some papers across the desk. "These are your copies to keep."

"Do you think it's all necessary?" Bill leafed through the pages.

"Definitely. Somebody tried to defraud you and we want to make sure they don't succeed. I don't want one of our oldest customers to be unhappy."

"Oldest customers?" Bill frowned. "I'm not that old."

Emil stood and held out his hand. "I know you're not. You're only a year older than me." He smiled at me. "We're not over the hill yet."

"Not by a long shot," I assured him—and Bill. "I'm right there on the hill with you."

"I appreciate you taking the time to handle this for me," Bill said as we walked toward the door. "I'm on my way to buy a computer today, so maybe I can figure out how to get online and check my accounts more closely."

"I can help with that." I plucked a brochure from a display as we ambled toward the door. "This should have all the information we need."

"It was nice meeting you, Miss Madison," Emil said as we paused by the back door. "Bill and Mary—what a classic combination."

"Nice meeting you, too." I took the offered hand. "And nice to meet a classmate of Bill's. I'll have to get him to pull out some scrapbooks for me to see."

"I'm not about to pull out those scrapbooks," Bill said as we emerged into the cold March sunshine. "That was *way* too long ago."

"Ah, come on. I'd like to see your press clippings."

"Maybe someday. So let's go spend some money. Where to?"

"Let's start with some office places then finish at the computer places."

"Sounds like a plan to me." He helped me back up into the truck. "Your wish is my command."

"Now there's an idea."

He laughed as we drove away.

It took four hours, but we finally settled on a desktop computer model. "Now you have to help me get it set up," he said. "There's probably miles of cords and cables."

I looked back into the truck where our purchases were safely stowed out of sight under the pickup bed cover. "Piece of cake," I said breezily. "It's all color-coded. We'll have you surfing the Internet in no time." I leaned against my side of the truck and regarded him as we drove west, the setting sun lighting our way. "This has been fun."

"It has been." He smiled at me, his dark blue eyes warm and happy. "I feel so comfortable with you. Usually I get all...well, nervous or something when I'm around women. I never know what to say or how to act."

I nodded agreement. "I know. I start to wonder if he thinks I'm good-looking or if he notices my wrinkles and my gray hair, or if—"

Bill made a snorting noise. "Wrinkles? What wrinkles? And that's not gray in your hair. Look at me!" He scowled at the road. "I've got white hair."

"I told you—men get distinguished, women get old."

"Not you. How old are you? Forty?"

I laughed. "I'm almost fifty. In just a few days. April Fool's Day."

"Not. And here I thought I was robbing the cradle."

"Nope. I'm an old lady."

"You're young enough for me."

My good mood was dampened as we drove through town and I glimpsed a sign on a low brick building. "Benteen's? What's that?"

"It's just a bar. I thought we'd go to Sparky's. They've got better food than Benteen's." He took a right at the corner and glanced at me. "I thought we'd stop there then go to the house and set up the computer. Is that okay with you?"

"Sure." I looked at the plain front door of the bar as we passed. I had to know. The indecision was gnawing at me. "Um, Bill."

"Hmm?" He looked at me then waved to someone walking on the sidewalk.

"I was talking to a guy who knows you." Before he could ask who, I said, "I'm sorry, I can't tell you who it was. Remember I said I do some counseling at the unemployment office? Well, it's somebody from there. It's confidential."

"Okay," he said cautiously, taking a left turn at the bank where we'd been that morning and heading toward a parking lot near a small strip mall. "Was there a problem? Did this guy say something?" He glanced at me when I didn't speak. "Come on, Threemie. I won't bite."

"Oh, that was a bad choice of words." Now that I chose this path, I wasn't sure how to walk down it without stubbing a toe. I decided just to take the plunge. "He said that a woman had complained about you because you were...rough. And that another woman said that you...took advantage of her."

67

Bill's face slowly suffused with color as he stared straight ahead. "Crystal," he spat through clenched lips. "That bitch." He pounded the steering wheel.

My stomach dropped when I heard the hatred in his voice.

Chapter 6

My startled look must have told him how I felt.

"I'm sorry, Threemie. I just hate it when rumors go flying around. It's always that way in a small town. Damn."

"Rumors?" I tried to unobtrusively slide even farther toward my door.

Bill caught sight of my movement. "I'm sorry, really. I didn't mean to sound like an ass—I didn't mean to get mad at you. It's just—" He sighed loudly and didn't say anything until he'd parked the truck. "I'd like to explain it to you. Can we go inside and talk?"

I nodded mutely. At least it was a public place. I opened the door and slid out before he could come around the truck to help me. He didn't say anything, just led the way to the building, where he jerked open the front door for me.

I peered around the murky interior of the bar, finally striking out for a booth against one wall, far away from the pool tables. As we sat down, I said, "Look, you don't owe me any explanations."

"No, no, it's just...well, embarrassing."

"I'm curious, that's all. It's odd to have somebody

say something like that. Especially somebody who's a stranger."

Bill looked up as the waitress approached, brandishing menus and drink coasters. He ordered a beer and I ordered wine. While the waitress vanished to get our drinks, I examined the menu, covertly looking at Bill's embarrassed expression. Why did Tim want me to know about it? What was there to know? I felt a tight knot of dismay start to form in my stomach. Maybe Bill was a bad guy after all. Let's face it, my instincts weren't always 100%—look at Jack, he'd been cheating on me for almost a year before I figured it out. Damn it, what was Bill hiding? Why did he look so guilty?

The waitress returned and we ordered burgers, fries, and more drinks. When she left, I faced Bill. "You don't have to tell me."

He cleared his throat. "It was just embarrassing, more for CiCi than for me, really. A few years ago we were all at a birthday party for one of the guys on the crew. We went to Benteen's. It's a hangout for folks from the factory. So we went there and CiCi—she worked there part-time—she got a bit drunk and she decided to do some dancing."

He paused so long I prompted, "And?"

Bill stared intently into his beer. "Well, she did this...thing." He gulped some beer and avoided looking at me. "On me."

"Ah." I nodded briskly, pieces of the puzzle clicking into place. "Lap dancing?"

He flushed. "Yeah. It was embarrassing because I didn't want her to. Then she started—" He gulped some more beer.

"Oh, dear," I said, seeing where this story was heading. "She started stripping?"

He nodded. "I didn't know what to do."

I could just imagine it. Poor Bill—poor sweet, sexy, handsome Bill—sitting there with some girl coming on to him in front of all his friends. "What did you do?" I asked, my stomach twisting in knots. *Well, duh. What do you think he did?* the little devil perched on my shoulder said. *Maybe nothing,* the little angel perched on my other shoulder admonished.

"I took her home." He gulped more beer. "I poured her into bed and called her sister. Marcy worked at the plant, too. She came over and stayed with CiCi."

I stared. "You didn't...?" Now it was my turn to down some booze.

He looked shocked. "She was drunk. She didn't know what she was doing."

I could visualize the scene in my head. "Oh, yes she did," I said in a low voice. "It was sweet of you to resist, though."

He looked uncomfortable. "It wouldn't have been right."

"But I'm sure she wanted you to—"

"Doesn't matter. She was drunk."

I looked down at the wine in my glass. "I guess I better be careful to never over-indulge around you, then. Otherwise you might just take me home and leave me." I raised my eyes slowly and met his across the table.

He smiled. "Yeah. You'd better be careful."

My heart started to hammer wildly. There was a lot of promise in his sultry look. I lifted my wine glass with trembling fingers and managed a swallow. "You mentioned somebody named Crystal, though. How does she factor into this?"

He leaned back in the booth, his face suddenly harsh. "I dated her for a while, a few years ago. She was into...rough stuff."

"Rough..." My voice trailed off as I processed what he'd said. "You mean BDSM?" His shocked look made me laugh. "Sorry, but I have heard of it." I leaned over the table and touched his hand.

Bill blew out a sigh then smiled wryly. "Yeah, I guess that's what it's called. It wasn't exactly what I was, um, good at. I guess you could say I didn't accommodate her." He raised his beer and took a long swallow.

I recognized a diversionary tactic when I saw it, but I decided not to press my luck. He'd been honest with me, or at least it sounded like he was honest. It wasn't my business to go prying any more into his life than I already had. If he wanted to share details with me, he could, and in his own time. "I guess that's what comes of living in small town, hmm? Everybody thinks they want to share in your business?"

He shook his head. "Crystal was always kind of wild. I wouldn't be surprised if she spread some rumors around. She wasn't happy when I broke up with her."

Was it really just a 'woman scorned' scenario? How would I know? Hell, I wouldn't know until we got to the point of no return. Damn, why couldn't this be easy? Why couldn't I just trust somebody?

He met my eyes with an honest, direct look and my panic started to subside. I raised my wine glass. "Here's to the past—long may it stay buried."

He raised his glass to mine. "I'll second that sentiment."

****

When we finished dinner and left the bar, a light snow was falling. Bill helped me into the truck then hesitated before closing the door. "Would you like to come back to my house and help me set up the system? I'll understand if you don't, given what...somebody is saying about me. But I'd like it if you would."

I looked down into his face. Snow had settled on his dark hair and it glinted in the parking lot lights.

"I'd like to go to your house."

He smiled and leaned in toward me. "Good." His kiss was quick but it still left me breathless. When he slid behind the steering wheel he held out his hand and I took it. "Thank you for trusting me." He raised my hand to his lips and kissed it.

I was so surprised I just gawked at him. He laughed and set my hand back on the seat. "You're a special person, Mary Margaret Madison. I hope you know it."

"Thanks for thinking so. I hope you don't mind I pried into your life."

"Not at all." He drove us past closed businesses and down a residential street not far from the bar. "A person has to be careful in today's world. Life isn't as easy as it was when we were growing up."

"No kidding. Somehow, along the way, it all got real complicated."

"Well, some things are still simple," he said as we drove down a tree-lined street, one that looked surprisingly like mine back in Hopkins. He glanced at me and smiled. "Boy meets girl. Boy likes girl. Boy wants to know girl a lot better."

I laughed at his mischievous look. "A lot better?"

"Oh yeah." He pulled into the driveway of a small two-story Cape Cod house with a small front yard and large trees silhouetted behind it.

I reached for the passenger side door handle but he stopped me by tugging on my arm. "Come out this side." He patted the seat he'd just vacated. I slid across the seat and he put his hands on my waist, slowly pulling me out of the truck, letting me slide against him as I did so. I ended up leaned back against the seat with Bill standing very close to me. "I've been thinking about doing this all day," he said, stepping forward.

His thighs pushed against mine. I slipped my arms inside his jacket and felt the solid warmth of his back. "You have?"

"Hmm." He lowered his head. "And this."

Our lips met and I held on for dear life as his body pressed against mine and his lips captured me. His lips were firm, hot, and insistent. Even as he kissed, his body moved against mine. I felt his big thighs, taut stomach, and another intriguing hardness press against me. My breasts flattened against his chest and my body softened, accepting him. He made a small noise of pleasure as my arms twined around his neck and he tightened his hold on me.

When we broke apart, Bill looked down at me, his eyes dark and mysterious. "You're one helluva good kisser, Mary Madison." He dipped his head to brush a kiss across my ear lobe.

"I was just thinking the same thing about you."

"Maybe we're a good match."

"I think we are."

He kissed me again, gentle and sweet. "Let's get my computer set up. Then relax a bit."

I looked into his smoldering eyes. "Sounds good to me." Relax, hell. If we had any more kisses like that one, relaxation was the last thing on my mind.

I took charge of the printer box while Bill grabbed the CPU box and we went into the house. A huge yellow cat greeted us at the door as we walked into the house. "That's Magoo," Bill said, setting down the box. He took off his jacket and went to a nearby closet then returned to me and took my coat. "I'll get the other boxes."

"Can I help?"

"Nope. I've got it. You go on in and get comfortable." He vanished back out the door.

I followed the big cat, who meandered through a kitchen and another doorway, which turned out to be a den. When I stooped to pet him, he broke into a house-rumbling purr and flopped down, exposing his white tummy. I looked at the new computer furniture in the corner of the den. "You did this right," I said as Bill came in with another box.

"I thought I should." He set the computer box on the floor next to the printer box I set down. "I want to be comfortable when I'm sending you email late at night."

I smiled at him. "Just pick up a phone and call."

"I don't have your number," he pointed out as he bent over the box.

"We can fix that."

He straightened up. Our eyes met and he smiled. "Good."

As I predicted, it didn't take long to hook up the computer. We got his ISP account activated, installed the printer, and ran a few test programs. An hour after we started I sat back in the chair. "All done. You'll need to do a bit of customizing, but you can do that as you use it."

"I'm impressed." Bill leaned over my shoulder and kissed me. "You're the greatest. I wouldn't have known how to do any of the computer stuff."

I waggled my eyebrows at him. "Told you I was a geek."

He touched my cheek. "A beautiful geek."

I blinked at him. "You're going to spoil me with such talk."

"Complaining?"

"Not at all."

He sank down in the armchair next to me. "Let me spoil you some more."

When we pulled apart several minutes later, I was sitting on his lap, my arms around his neck. "How'd that happen?" I murmured into the scratchy skin of his jaw.

He shivered. "Just lucky, I guess. I've never met anybody like you before." He ran his hands over my back. "Part of me wants to just keep on kissing you until..." He blushed.

"Until?"

"You know." He looked at me, his eyes intent. "But I really want to know you. I want to go slow, Threemie. I want to make sure this..." He shook his head. "I don't know what I'm trying to say."

I ran a hand over his cheek, feeling the day's growth of beard. "You're saying you want to see if this is more than just a fling kind of thing."

He kissed me. "Exactly."

I put my head on his shoulder. "Good. I'm willing to wait, too." I looked up at him and winked. "Not for too long, though."

He hugged me. "No. Not for too long."

I wasn't anxious to break this magic spell, but I knew if I didn't, things might progress too far and too fast. I wasn't ready for that yet. "Show me your cars. Do you work on them here? Or do you rent another place somewhere?"

"Nope, I built the garage in back. I just walk out there whenever I feel like it and go to work." His hands lingered on me. "Want to see it?"

"Yep. And I would like to see the rest of your house." I glanced at him. "Maybe you can show me the upstairs some other time?"

"You bet I will."

I heard the promise in his voice. I tugged him to his feet and he gave me a quick tour of the kitchen, living room, den, tiny dining room and bathroom on the first floor. When I headed for the coat closet, he shook his head. "You won't need it. I've got a heated walkway between the house and the garage."

I followed him out the back door. "Heated garage?"

He put an arm around my shoulders, holding me against him. "I like my comforts."

"I'll remember that in the future." I preceded him through the door at the end of the short walkway. Bill reached around me to flip the switch and the shop sprang into light.

"Wow." I looked around the immaculate, well-lit space. It wasn't at all what I expected. When he said he worked on cars, I thought...oil, grease, dirt and... I looked back at Bill, who'd walked to a tidy workbench against one wall near a couch, TV, and armchair in the corner. "This is very cool."

"It's my current project." He gestured to the Mustang in the center of the space. I walked forward, looking at the navy Mustang, smiling slowly.

"Neat car." I stepped over tires, a toolbox, and a pile of fenders. "I used to date a guy who had one like this. His was dark green, though. 1966, isn't it?"

Bill nodded. I ran a hand over the finish. "Custom white interior?"

He nodded, hands deep into his jeans pockets, watching me circle the car. I leaned over and looked into the back seat. I gave him a good view of my ass then I straightened up and shot him an assessing look over one shoulder. "I have fond memories of a car just like this one." I moved to stand next to him and lean against the workbench. "*Very* fond memories."

He looked down into my eyes. "The back seat isn't big enough for *very* fond memories."

I snorted with disdain. "Depends. The back seat is big enough if you're motivated. And if you're agile."

He laughed. "You sound like you speak from experience."

"Oh, I do. I do indeed." I glanced around the garage and saw the bright red Ford pickup in the dark back corner. "Holy shit. Look at that. What year is it?"

Bill flipped on the lights in the corner as I crossed the garage and put a hand on the rear bed sideboard. "1953. It's an F100."

I stood on my tiptoes and peeked inside. "Man, look at this. This truck looks brand new." I peered back over my shoulder at him. "You're an artist. Look at the dash—and the radio! It's all so new looking."

"You can get inside." He crossed the room and opened the driver side door.

I pulled out of the window and looked at him. "Really?"

"Hop in."

"Wow." I got into the truck, settling myself behind the wheel. "This is so beautiful." I touched the immaculate dashboard, the steering wheel, and the cloth seats. "Bill, this is so cool. How long did it take? It must have taken forever."

He shrugged. "A year or two. I only worked on it now and then. It was hard to find parts then I had to find somebody to do the seats just right for me."

I ran a hand over the red and gray cloth of the seats. "Do you ever take it out?"

"Sure. For shows and rallies. You should go with me sometime. A bunch of us get together and show off our wheels. Only during the summer months, of course," he added. "I don't like to take it out in the snow."

I ran my hands around the steering wheel. "I didn't realize people could do things like this." I reluctantly slid out of the cab. "It's like a work of art."

"We'll take it out this spring." He looped an arm around my shoulders. "Go for a drive in the park."

I steered us back to the Mustang. "Get this baby ready, and we'll take it out, too." I nudged him with my hip.

Bill looked down and kissed the tip of my nose. "Deal. Now *that's* motivation!" He glanced at the clock over the workbench and I followed his gaze, amazed to see it was almost nine o'clock.

"I'd better be getting home." I took one last lingering look around the workshop. "This is such a nice place," I said as we walked back to the house. "It's so comfortable. You can curl up with a good book or work on your cars or...well, it's just so nice."

"Can I talk you into staying a bit longer?" Bill enfolded me in his arms as we entered the house. "Just a bit?"

I hugged him tightly. He felt so good, so strong, and warm and *male*. It was oh so tempting to stay there, but things were moving fast enough for me. I didn't want to go any faster.

Bill must have sensed my reluctance because he leaned back to look down at me. "You're right. Let's take it easy." He helped me on with my coat and led the way outside to his truck. "You should come over sometime and keep me company," he said, giving me a hand up into the cab. "You can bring something to read, and I'll put on some music and we'll...work." He leaned in and looked at me.

"I'd love to. I have a bunch of gardening and golf magazines to get caught up on. I'll bring them and read while you do your car thing."

"Great." He hurried around to the driver's side and clambered into the cab. "Maybe we can have lunch."

"That sounds good. I could cook. I make a mean pot of soup. I'll put it on in the morning in the crockpot then we can go to my house for dinner at night." I had a mental pause. I was asking him to my house. Should I? Oh, hell, yes. "I'd like to cook dinner."

"I'd like to cook breakfast for you." He stared at me with warm dark eyes.

"You big old flirt, you." I touched his face. "Let's give it a little time, okay? I'm not *quite* ready for such a big step."

"I know. But...I just wanted you to know how I feel."

"I feel the same way. But for now..."

He patted the seat next to him. "Care to join me?"

I scooted over to sit next to him on the bench seat. He put the truck into gear and started driving back toward town. "Can I pick you up tomorrow?" he asked, putting his arm around my shoulders.

"Sure. I'll give you detailed instructions on how to get there. And I'll give you my various phone numbers." He grinned and I nudged him. "What?"

"In for a penny, in for a pound."

"I guess so." I looked out at the snowy landscape. "I feel like I know you so well. And I do trust you."

"It's a tough step to take if you've been divorced or hurt in the past." His hand tightened on my shoulder. "Thank you. I won't let you down."

"You say all the right things. It should scare me, but it doesn't."

"What time can I pick you up tomorrow? I usually work out at the gym in the morning on Sunday because it's not busy then. How about afterwards? At ten or so?"

"I usually work out, too. Talk about two peas in a pod. If I work out through the winter, I can golf one heck of a lot better in the spring."

"No kidding. I hate the first time out on the course when your muscles are screaming."

"I'm in an indoor golf league, so it helps a lot, too. We have our big final tournament starting this week. You should come and watch us."

"Indoor golf? Where?"

"There's one of those simulation places over in Bloomington. We have a ladies' golf league and we play from January to April. It's a blast. We eat pizza, drink beer, and golf." I beamed at him. "What better way to pass the wintertime in Minnesota?"

He laughed. "No kidding. And you're having a tournament?"

"Yep. Eliminations start on Tuesday night and the finals are in April. Come and watch."

"I think I will." He squeezed my shoulder again. "Why don't we get together tomorrow morning? You can come to my gym and work out. Then we'll go to my place and spend the afternoon puttering around together."

I raised an eyebrow. "Puttering around?"

"Somehow that didn't come out quite the way I meant it." He glanced down at me and smiled. "Maybe it did. One of those Freudian slips."

"It might be fun to work out together. But I warn you, I'm not a jock or anything. Just a little weight lifting and a bit of biking."

We got to the parking garage and he drove inside. "Which floor?"

"Two." I straightened up, peering around the half-full garage. Bill drove up the ramp and I pointed. "There."

An empty slot was available across from my car so he parked his truck and opened his door. He paused, staring at Stella, then came to my side of the truck and helped me out. I followed his gaze to my car.

"What happened?" I leaned over, looking down at the tires. The back two tires were completely flat. "They're totally pancaked! Did I run over something in the road?"

Bill knelt by the back tire and touched the rubber. "They're slashed, Threemie. This isn't just a flat." He looked up at me, his eyes troubled. "Somebody did this on purpose."

## Chapter 7

I straightened. "Why would somebody do—?" Then I remembered. "Oh, no."

Bill put his hands on my shoulders. "What is it?"

"Oh, man." I stared up at him. "It can't be."

"Threemie?" He shook me gently. "What is it?"

I gulped back tears. "I might have seen something during the murder the other night. I went to the police and reported it and..." I wasn't sure what to say. "It might be a cop who's involved." I told him about my evening with Detective Sloan and the police artist. Bill listened, his hands running soothingly over my shoulders.

He finally pulled me into an embrace, cradling me against his chest. "It's okay. You're safe."

I sniffed against his flannel shirt. "What should I do?"

Bill looked over my head to my crippled car. "We call the detective. Let him handle this. Do you have his phone number?'

I pulled away from his warm comfort to scrabble through my purse, finally finding Sloan's business card. I thrust it at Bill.

Bill took the card and led me back to his truck.

"You sit here and I'll call him."

I started to agree then realized what I was doing. "You can't get involved with this." I grabbed for the card in his hand.

Bill lifted his arm, easily keeping the card out of my reach. "What do you mean?"

"This might be dangerous." I reached for the business card waving over his head. "You can't get involved. I shouldn't have told you anything. You could get hurt."

"Threemie." He put his arms around me, pinning my arms at my sides. "I'm involved if you're involved. End of discussion."

"But—"

Bill kissed me, a slow, melting kiss that made my bones go limp and the blood thud in my ears. "I'm involved." Before I knew what was happening, he'd tucked me into the passenger seat then turned away and pulled out his cell phone, leaning against the closed door. I couldn't roll down the windows because they were electric, and I couldn't hear through the glass. I leaned back against the seat and let tears trickle down my cheeks. I didn't want him getting in trouble because of me. Shit, I should have kept my mouth closed. Now he'd be involved.

I looked at Bill, pacing toward Stella and staring at it as he talked into the phone. I felt like I'd known him forever and knew just about everything about him. Well, everything except for...I eyed his long legs, strong chest, and his small, tight butt. How could I think of sex at a time like this? He turned and looked at me. Our eyes met and he smiled a big Dimple Fest at me. Well, that answered that question.

Bill closed the phone and came back to the truck. I opened the door to hear him. "He's on his way. He told us to wait for him here."

I nodded. "Was he grumpy? He was grumpy last

night."

Bill smiled. "Yep." He went around to the driver's side and got in. "Come over here. I'll keep you warm while we wait."

I slid across the seat and huddled into the strength of Bill's embrace. "I'm sorry."

He pressed me against him. "Nothing to be sorry for. This just means I get to drive you home."

"But—"

"Threemie, I care about what happens to you." He looked down at me, smoothing back my flyaway hair. "It doesn't matter I've only known you a few days. You're important to me. I'm not going to desert you now. I'll stick with you on this."

I stared into his deep blue eyes and felt as though I was falling into his heart. "You're so nice to me. I'm lucky you chased me out of the bar."

He blushed. "You'll never let me forget that, will you? You'll remind me of it forever, won't you?"

"Yep." I leaned my head into the crook of his shoulder.

"Good." He kissed the top of my head and held me against him. "I'll hold you to that promise. Forever."

\*\*\*\*

Marcus Sloan was royally pissed off and I could see it. I sighed when I saw him get out of the big police sedan. "He's grumpy."

"I get the feeling it's a perpetual state of mind with him," Bill commented. He got out of the driver's side while I climbed out of the passenger side of the truck. We approached Sloan, who was staring down at the wounded Subaru with a disgusted look on his face.

"Who'd you tell you were coming here?" he demanded when I neared him.

Bill opened his mouth to speak but I said quickly, "Good evening to you, too, Detective Sloan.

Yes, it is upsetting my car was vandalized. No, I doubt if anyone I know did it. Perhaps you know someone who did?" I shot him a narrow-eyed glare.

He glanced at Bill. "You're the boyfriend?" His glance slid to me. "Correction—the gentleman friend?"

Bill held out his hand. "Bill Manion." Sloan shook his hand then turned back to Stella.

"No one knew I was parking here," I said. "A friend knew I was meeting Bill today, but not that I was parking here." I rolled my eyes. "Damn. I should call Kate. She's probably got an ulcer by now." I smiled apologetically at Bill. "Checking in."

"Smart." Bill watched me step away from the car and pull out my cell phone. I kept an ear tuned to him as I dialed Kate's number.

"She told me about yesterday and the police artist," Bill said in a low voice.

Sloan glowered at me. "Blabby of her."

"Maybe. Do you think this is related?"

"Kate, this is Threemie."

"Oh, thank God. I was going to call the police if I didn't hear from you soon. Are you okay? Where are you? Did—"

I tuned her out and watched Sloan kneel by the tire and examine it. "Somehow I don't think it's just random vandalism," he commented. "And somehow I don't think she's got a lot of enemies." He stood up and shook his head. "Nobody's got her name except me and a captain in the Hennepin County PD. Nobody should even know she's involved in a murder investigation."

"I'm fine, fine. I'm in Chaska. I had a bit of car trouble."

"Car trouble? What? I thought this guy was a mechanic? Why can't he..."

"She's not really involved in a murder investigation, is she?" Bill said quietly as Sloan continued prowling around the car. "Are you going to look for fingerprints?"

Sloan glanced at me and I pretended disinterest as I tried to placate Kate. "Not that kind of car trouble. I've got a flat tire. Actually, I've got two. I'll call you tomorrow and fill you in. Everything's fine, though, Kate. Just fine."

"Two flats? What happened?"

"Okay, it looks like somebody did it on purpose."

"Threemie! If you're having—"

"Talk to you later." I folded the phone and joined Sloan and Bill as Sloan said, "I don't know if I want to bring attention to this. I'll call in a favor or two, have the guys at the impound garage look it over for me. I'll call a guy on the forensics team and ask him to take a look." Sloan glanced at Bill, leaning against the low concrete wall in front of the car. "I'm worried about an official report."

Bill nodded. "Yeah. I can see that."

"I want to make sure she's safe." Sloan glanced at me.

"She wants to be sure she's safe, too," I snapped.

"I'll take Threemie home tonight," Bill said, shooting me a quelling look. "And she'll be with me all day tomorrow."

Sloan considered it. "I'll have somebody keep an eye on her house tonight. What are you doing tomorrow?" Bill outlined our plans to go to the gym then go to his house. Sloan nodded. "Let me know if the plans change."

"I'll take you to the airport tomorrow to rent a car," Bill said to me. "It's the only rental spot open on Sunday."

"What? Can't we just put on the spare and..." I stared at the two flats. "Oh. Right. Two tires." I looked at Sloan. "Is this part of that thing?"

Sloan shrugged. He looked small and solid next to Bill's long, rangy length. "Maybe. I'm going to have it towed to impound and the forensic guys will look it over. We should have it back to you tomorrow. You might not need a rental."

"We'll see." Bill put an arm around me. "Why don't I take you home now? We'll let Detective Sloan handle this."

"I'll call you later and let you know what I find." It was a clear dismissal and I straightened, prepared to give Sloan a blast of wrath.

"Okay," Bill said. "We'll talk to you later."

I opened my mouth to speak but closed it when Bill maneuvered me into the passenger seat of the truck. I glared at Sloan, who was talking on his cell phone. "He's so damn bossy."

Bill climbed into the driver's side. "It's his job." He backed the truck out of its slot and drove out of the garage, watching Sloan in the rear view mirror. He held out an arm and I scooted across the seat near him. "Tell me how to get to your place."

I glanced back once at my car then turned back to face front. "I don't feel right about just leaving it."

"It's okay."

"You're pretty calm about this."

"Nothing to get worried about. We'll let Sloan do his job and see what he finds out." Bill's hand tightened on my shoulder. "Directions?"

Half an hour later we pulled into my driveway. I hopped out of the truck and led the way to the doorway at the side of the garage. "I usually just use the garage door opener," I said as I fumbled for keys in my purse. "I hope I can figure out which key works." I opened the door and preceded him into the empty garage, up the steps, and into the kitchen where the resident tyrants awaited us.

"Sorry, guys." I set my purse on the counter. "I got delayed."

Bill leaned over to let the cats sniff his hands then he removed his shoes, leaving them on the rug near the door and following me into the living room. "Nice place."

I followed his gaze to the overstuffed furniture, wood floors and large windows. "I like it." I took off my coat and tossed it on the dining room chair. "There's a small park back there so no one can build behind me." I gestured to the windows then looked at him. "Take off your coat. Want some coffee? A beer?" I headed back to the kitchen and Bill followed me, leaning in the doorway and watching as I looked in the fridge.

"Beer would be nice, if you don't mind me staying a while."

I looked up, startled. "Mind? I'm counting on it."

He shucked off his coat, tossing it on a kitchen chair. "Then beer it is."

I emerged from the fridge with a bottle and a carafe of wine. "Old Peculiar?" I asked, hefting the bottle.

"Great."

"Grab the chips." I gestured toward the cupboard over the stove. We went into the living room, settling on the couch overlooking the park behind my house.

Bill propped his feet up on the hassock. Muffin sniffed Bill's hair from a perch on the back of the couch and Snuggle settled herself on the arm of the couch where she could examine him. "They're just curious," I said. "That's Major Muffin and she's Sgt. Snuggle."

"You were Army?"

"Jack was. He named 'em. I got them in the divorce." I sipped my wine. "He got the buxom young girl."

"Stupid man. But his loss is my gain."

"Yeah. How about that?" I leaned against him. "What a weird day." I held up my wine glass and Bill clinked his mug against its rim.

"Here's to our future," he said, looking down at me.

"I'll drink to that." I sipped my wine. "Why would someone slash the tires?"

"Maybe Sloan can figure it out," Bill said, staring out at the dark night.

"I meant what I said earlier, Bill. I don't want to get you involved. This might be dangerous stuff."

He took my glass and set it on the end table next to his mug of beer. Then he put his arms around me and pulled me down on the couch with him. "Let's get involved," he suggested, stretching out.

"You old flirt, you." I snuggled into his left arm and slung a leg over his.

"Nice couch."

I looked up as he looked down. Our lips met in a slow, languid, gentle kiss building in intensity until my legs ended up clutching his thigh and my body was so hot I wondered why I didn't ignite in his arms.

I inched upward a bit more and my sweater inched with me. Bill tentatively put a hand on the bare skin of my side and began a gentle stroking. I shivered at his touch, arching against him. "Bill?"

"Hmm?"

"Your offer to cook breakfast is sounding really good."

I think it took a minute for my words to sink in. When they did, Bill looked down at me, startled. "You barely know me."

"And vice versa," I pointed out. I ran my hands over his flannel-shirted chest then wiggled a bit against his hip, tucking my leg between his.

He looked into my eyes. "I know you, Mary Margaret."

I ran the back of my hand over his raspy cheek. "I know you, too, Bill Irishman."

The ringing telephone caused Major Muffin to

jump from his viewing perch on the couch with a hiss. I rolled my eyes in exasperation. "It's probably Mr. Grumpy."

Bill reached out an arm to grab the phone from the charging cradle on the end table. He held it out for me.

"This is Threemie."

"Threemie? What's that?"

"I was right. It's Mr. Grumpy." I grinned as Bill kissed the tip of my nose. "This is Mary Madison."

"What's with Threemie?" Sloan demanded.

"It's a nickname. Do you have something to tell me?" I settled more comfortably against Bill, propping the phone against one shoulder so my hand could stray over his chest, toying with the buttons on his shirt.

"The forensic guys are working on your car tonight. They got some prints and we'll run 'em. I can bring it over to you in the morning. What time are you and Manion going out?"

"What time are we leaving tomorrow?" I asked Bill.

"I'm picking you up at nine. And we're spending the day together." *And maybe the night*, his warm gaze said.

I smiled at him. "We're leaving at nine in the morning," I said into the phone. "I don't know what time I'll be back tomorrow night." I snuggled against Bill's warm, long length.

"I'll drop the car off in the morning. I've got a patrol unit driving by your place tonight. They'll keep an eye on things tomorrow, too. If you and Manion change your plans, call me." He hung up before I could agree or disagree.

"Yes, mother," I snapped, turning off the phone and dropping it on the floor. I turned my attention back to Bill. "He's coming by in the morning with my car."

"Hmm. I suppose that means I should go so you can get some rest."

I nodded, playing with the buttons of his shirt. "I suppose. In a few minutes."

He tugged me down on top of him. "In a few minutes," he agreed.

Half an hour later, Bill reluctantly disentangled himself. "I really have to go. If I don't..." He didn't have to finish the thought. If he didn't, I'd probably tear off his clothing for him.

We got up, arms entwined around each other, and moved toward the kitchen. "I'll be here early in the morning," he reminded me. "And you make sure to lock up behind me."

I nodded. "Don't worry. I always lock up." I watched as he put on his jacket and slipped into his shoes. "I had a great time today." Then I remembered. "Except for the part about the slashed tires."

Bill pulled me into his arms. "I'm going to call you when I get home. I want to make sure you're okay."

I snuggled against him, secretly pleased. "I'll be fine."

"Maybe. But I'm still going to call. So you go get ready for bed and tuck yourself in. I'll call and say good night."

"Okay." I stood on tiptoes to kiss him quickly. "Good night." I peeked out the kitchen window as he clambered into his truck and backed out of the drive. I waved and he flashed his bright lights as he drove down the street. With a sigh, I locked the outside and inside doors, turned off the lights, and meandered into the living room, where I flopped down on the couch and stared at the ceiling.

Good heavens, who would have thought I would find a man at this stage of life? Middle age had a lot of fierce competition out there. I scowled as I remembered the chickie who'd taken Jack. Then I started to smile. She'd be hitting thirty soon. There was justice in the world. Here I was, in middle age, and I had this hot, sexy man in my life. Hell, Jack wasn't so hot when he was thirty, much less in his fifties.

I wandered down the hall to the bathroom. "Lord have mercy," I commented to Snuggles, who was dozing in the bathtub. "That man ignites me every time he touches me." I considered it as I washed my face, smeared on my nightly face cream, and brushed my teeth. I felt weak and almost dizzy with desire. I walked down the hall to the bedroom, yawning as I stripped off my clothing and dropped it on the chair. Major Muffin had already staked out his spot in the center of the double bed as I pulled on my sleep T-shirt and got between the sheets.

The phone next to the bed rang. Was Bill calling so soon? "Hello?"

It was a woman's voice. "Are you stupid? Tim told you to be careful about him and there you were, letting him paw you! What are you, retarded?"

I sat bolt upright in bed, shocked. "What?"

"We tried to warn you. He's playing with you, like he did with me. Did you ask him? He used me then he walked away. He told people I was a slut. He ruined my reputation."

"Now wait a minute!" I struggled to drag the covers around me. "You're lying! I talked to Bill about it. It wasn't anything like that."

"And you believed him? Maybe you're just desperate for a man. "

I sputtered with outrage. "How dare you! Who are you? Why are you doing this? What's Bill ever done to you? You coward, how dare you—"

The phone went quiet in my hand. I panicked, afraid the line had gone completely dead. Then I breathed a sigh of relief when the dial tone clicked on. I slammed the phone down into the cradle. Why was someone picking on Bill? Who wanted to smear him? I flopped back on the bed, glaring at the ceiling.

Several minutes later the phone rang again. I eyed it warily then finally picked it up. "Are you in bed?" Bill asked.

I tried to take a deep breath to still my pounding heart. Sgt. Snuggle leapt up on the bed and I almost jumped through the roof in surprise. "Damn cat," I muttered.

"Are you okay?" Bill asked. "Is everything all right?"

I took another deep breath. "I'm fine. I guess I'm a bit...scared." I ached to ask, *What's going on? Who's got a grudge against you? What the hell is happening?*

"I felt bad leaving you alone, but...I guess I didn't want to rush things, either."

The acid words rushed back into my brain. *He likes it rough.* "There's the murder thing, then meeting you and..." I shook my head. "So much is changing all of a sudden." I wondered if my explanation sounded as weak to him as it did to me.

"It bothered you, didn't it? Did you believe me about CiCi? I told you the truth."

I nodded into the darkness. "I believe you. But...why would someone want to hurt you? Why would they want to make me think bad things about you? I don't understand it."

"I don't either, Threemie. I guess you just have to trust your instincts on me."

"Yeah, but..." What if the phone call was right? What if... No. No. I may not know a lot about men, but Bill was just what he seemed—nice, gentle, and kind.

"I wish I knew who's spreading rumors about me."

"Or maybe..." I wedged my pillow more comfortably under me. "How many people knew what happened when you took that girl home?"

"Huh?"

"How many people know you and she didn't— you know?"

"I'm not sure. It was bad enough she made a fool of herself in front of people. The only way to get her to stop was to get her out of there. I suppose people thought..."

"Maybe somebody thinks you and CiCi slept together, but he doesn't know the truth."

"Well, hell, it was years ago!" Bill said in disgust. "It's nobody's business."

I nodded. That was it. Somebody thought they had the truth and they didn't. "You're right. It's all in the past and it doesn't matter."

"You mean it?"

"Of course I do. Honestly, Bill. I trust you."

"Good. I'll see you in the morning."

"I'll put the soup in the crockpot and we'll have dinner here tomorrow night."

"That sounds great. Threemie?"

"Hmm?"

"Do you believe in love at first sight?"

I caught my breath. "I don't know."

He sighed. "I do. Good night."

I hung up the phone slowly. I had a hard time getting to sleep.

Chapter 8

I overslept until seven-thirty and shot out of bed like a bat out of hell. My bed head was tamed with a quick shower then I got to work on the potatoes, onion, and bacon for the soup. Just as I was transferring everything to the crockpot, the phone rang. I glanced at the clock—eight-thirty. I considered letting the answering machine pick up but it might be Bill, so I juggled the mixing bowl and the phone.

"It's Threemie."

"Are you going to explain that Threemie thing?" Sloan demanded.

"I'm busy right now," I said through clenched teeth. "Can you make this fast?"

"I'm on the way over with your car. The squad who patrolled will give me a ride back to the station."

"Someone patrolled all night?" I tried to peer out the kitchen window but gave up when I almost dropped my skillet.

"They drove through the neighborhood off and on. I'll be there in a few minutes. Is the gentleman friend there yet?"

I rolled my eyes. "He's on his way."

"Well, don't leave until I get there. We need to chat." He hung up.

I finished the potato soup as the phone rang again. "Are you sure you should go out with him today?" Kate demanded without so much as a 'hey there, hello'. "I thought about it all night and I'm not sure if you should. The tire thing is scary. Maybe it has to do with him. What if—"

"Good morning," I said. "Yes, I'm going out with him. No, I'm not worried."

"I should meet him. We all should. Your friends, that is."

I silently counted to five. "Sure. Maybe at the tournament?"

"Tournament?" I heard Martha, Kate's partner, shout out *golf tournament, remember?* "Oh, yeah," Kate said. "Tuesday, right? Okay, you bring him there and we'll all look him over."

"If he wants to come to the tournament, I'll be happy to have him. But no way are you and a bunch of work people going to give him the third degree."

"We just want—"

My Palm Pilot chimed from my purse, reminding me I was on Crisis Cell duty. I dug out the phone and clipped it to my waistband where it could thump me if I was needed. I heard a sound outside. I stood on tiptoes to look through the curtains and saw Bill's dark green truck pulling in to the driveway. "Gotta go. Talk to you later."

"Threemie, you have to—"

I hung up the phone and hurried to the door just as Bill was getting out of his truck. I tossed open the door. "Hey there." I almost swooned at the sight of him. He was so tall, dark, and handsome. Seriously. And when his dimples made an appearance I almost dropped to the ground and salivated.

He kicked through last night's snow to meet me,

but before he'd gone far, Marcus Sloan pulled into the driveway in Stella. I met Bill halfway, looping an arm around his waist and we walked to meet Sloan, who was getting out of the Subaru.

"Good as new," he said, holding out the keys.

"Where'd you get the tires?" I asked. Bill took the keys and walked toward my car.

"You owe me," Sloan said. "I've got a friend who owns a tire store. He opened up for me late last night."

"My insurance will cover it." I watched Bill as he stooped, looked at the tires, the fender, inside the car, and finally ended up standing next to Sloan.

"All okay?" Sloan asked.

Bill shrugged. "Pop the hood and I'll tell you."

Sloan looked skeptical but reached into the car and pulled the hood lever. Bill propped open the hood and leaned over the car. Fascinated, I leaned with him. "What are you looking for?" I asked, staring down at the maze of wires, metal gizmos, and odd gadgets.

He reached in and tugged some wires, touched a cap, and looked at some other parts I thought were the battery and possibly oil. "Just making sure nothing's out of place." He straightened and let the lid slam shut. He glanced at Sloan. "Find anything?"

"Can we go inside?" Marcus Sloan glanced around the quiet neighborhood. "My ride's coming in a few minutes."

I led the way into the house, watching with approval as Bill slipped out of his shoes and disapproval as Marcus Sloan walked into my kitchen without pausing at the front door rug to knock off the snow. "Smells good," Sloan said. "Soup?"

I nodded. "What did you find?"

Sloan leaned against the counter and crossed his arms over his chest. "We only found one set of prints near the tires. You wash the car lately?"

"I don't remember. I try to take it in at least once a month in the winter. It was probably clean last week."

"It looks like a utility knife or box opener was used," Sloan said. "It was something very sharp. There aren't any cameras in the garage. Who knew you guys would be out?" Sloan's baby blue gaze swung from me to Bill.

"Nobody," Bill said. "We had shopping to do then our plans were fluid afterwards."

I nodded agreement. "No one knew. What about the picture I did?" I sidled closer to Bill and he put an arm around my shoulders.

"The picture our *artist* did is being circulated," Sloan snapped. "Quietly."

"I've been thinking about this," Bill said. "From what Threemie told me, it sounds like there might be a cop involved."

"What is it with the Threemie thing?"

"You're avoiding the question," I pointed out.

Sloan shifted position, staring at his boots for a long minute then he raised his eyes to meet mine. "Yeah, it might be. I'm figuring it has to be somebody who knew Jimmy Van. He was the guy who was killed. He was Hmong and working undercover. It had to be somebody who benefited from Jimmy's death."

"Was it drugs, like I thought?"

Sloan pursed his lips then shook his head. "Jimmy was in Vice, which is where I met him. Every suburban police department has an officer who acts as liaison with the main metro departments. I'm the Vice liaison for Hopkins."

"And..." Bill prompted. "What was Vice doing working a case in Chaska?"

"Jimmy was the lead man in a task force established to investigate a teenage prostitution ring. The girls are brought over from the homeland—usually Laos and Thailand—to live with relatives. Then the family is pressured to make 'restitution' for the plane flight, money, clothing, and other advances used to get the girls into the country. The girls have to work for two years. At the end of the time, the debt is cleared." Sloan glared at my kitchen wall, his thoughts obviously elsewhere. "Of course, it never works out that way. Once a girl is in the life, it's almost impossible to get her out. They call it 'voluntary' prostitution."

I straightened indignantly. "Voluntary? What girl would volunteer? Those aren't women, they're children. They're probably scared, in a foreign country, afraid their families will be harmed. What idiot..." Bill's hand tightened on my shoulder and I looked up at him, surprised by the thoughtful look he and Sloan were exchanging.

"I remember," Bill said softly.

Sloan nodded. "Viet Nam."

"What? When?" I looked from one man to the other.

Bill shrugged. "The whores in 'Nam. Those girls were fifteen, sixteen years old, too." He grimaced. "I wasn't much older, but it still doesn't make it right. They were scared and hungry and afraid for their families, too."

Sloan ran a hand through his close-cropped gray and white hair. "Yeah. I remember."

Good heavens. This was one of those war stories no one ever talked about. I read about 'Nam, of course, and had even done my bit to protest it, but I hadn't known anyone who fought there who talked about, well, the 'other side' of war.

"It was a different lifetime ago," Bill said. "But I'm more concerned about this lifetime. Who knows Mary's involved in all of this?"

"Nobody. Your personal information is locked in my desk." He gave me a considering look. "Who the hell learns six languages?"

"Six languages?" Bill looked at me.

Sloan ticked them off on his fingers. "French, Arabic, Spanish, Dutch, German, Cantonese."

"Don't forget English."

"Yeah. Right, I forgot. Our mother tongue. Seven languages." He grinned then his expression sobered. "The only person I've shared the information with is Captain Salisbury, of the Vice Division for Hennepin County, Jimmy Van's boss. I'm not taking any chances with my potential star witness." He glanced out the window as I heard a car pull up. "My ride's here. Call if your plans change for today."

"What aren't you telling us?" Bill asked quietly.

"A lot," Sloan snapped. He straightened up, staring at Bill then coming to some kind of decision. "Look, I'll be straight with you. This has to be somebody who knows me and knows I work with Vice because somebody looked into my log files last night. On Friday I filed a report that a PW— Probable Witness—and I checked in at downtown headquarters to talk with a police sketch artist." He held up a hand when I started to talk. "It's standard procedure. If you'll recall, I had to sign in at the desk."

I nodded, remembering Friday night and the elevator ride. "And I saw the round-faced man and he must have seen me with you."

Sloan nodded. "I also had a notation for last night when I started on shift at one in the afternoon and was off at one this morning."

"Long shift," Bill commented.

Sloan's blue eyes met Bill's dark blue ones. "Yeah. I also noted I was out from ten-thirty last night until midnight."

"So?" I shrugged. "That's harmless, right?"

"I double-checked the logs for all the suburbs

last night. The impound officer reported the vandalism to your car last night. It's unusual. Usually the officer who has the car towed to impound files the report." He hesitated a long moment. "They filed your license plate number and a note indicating the tires were slashed."

"Shit," Bill said softly.

Sloan nodded. "Yeah. Anybody in police headquarters can access the DMV database." His gaze swung to me. "I think we have to assume they know your address and your car, now. If they don't, they will soon."

"Well, shit," I echoed.

"And I'm guessing you're not going to volunteer police protection," Bill said.

"What? Why not?" I stiffened, glaring at Sloan. "How come?"

"You should have been a cop," Sloan said. "You've got the mind for it."

Bill smiled. "I had my fill of shooting in 'Nam. You don't want to tip your hand, right? You're still trying to figure out who this guy is."

"Yep. I'll have patrol keep an eye on the house and I'll see to it you've got somebody watching out for you. That's why I need to know if your schedule changes."

"Not a problem." Bill pushed away from the counter and I straightened with him. "It just means I won't let Threemie out of my sight." He grinned down at me. "Not a bad assignment."

"My bodyguard," I simpered.

Sloan looked disgusted. "It won't be for long. I'm working on a plan to get this guy out in the open. Until then, I'll need your phone number, address, and cell phone number."

Bill told him then said, "We're going to work out at the gym then have a quiet day at my place. We'll probably come back here and eat an early dinner.

Then—what? A movie? A video?"

I nodded. "Sounds good."

Sloan went to the front door. "Keep me in the loop. I'll talk to you tonight," he said to me.

I glared at him. "That won't be necessary."

"I'll decide if it's necessary or not," Sloan said. "Have fun." He disappeared out the front door, closing it with a hearty slam behind him.

"Mr. Grumpy." I turned to Bill, who was regarding me with bemusement.

"He's just jealous."

I stared at him, gape-mouthed. "Not."

"Yep." Bill pulled me into his arms, pushing me back against the kitchen counter. "He wishes he was standing here with you. Like this." He pressed against me, his thighs insistent and the delicious hardness in his middle pressing against my belly. He bent his head and started to kiss my neck. "He's just jealous. And I can't blame him."

I ran my hands under his jacket, feeling the muscles in his back under the flannel shirt. "I'm looking forward to our day."

"Good. So am I." He kissed me, his hands roaming over me until I was squirming. "Damn, you get me bothered," he murmured when we finally pulled apart.

"The feeling's mutual." I put my arm through his. "Let's go work out. My regular gym clothes are in my locker at my gym so I just tossed in a T-shirt and some shorts."

Bill picked up my gym bag and I grabbed my book bag full of magazines and took one last look around the kitchen. "Why don't we just take my car? It's blocking your truck anyway and we'll come back here to eat later. What movie should we rent tonight?"

He smiled at me as I led the way out the door. "Something romantic?"

"Aw, rats. I wanted an action movie."

He laughed. "Different kind of action, maybe."

****

Somebody was after me. The thought kept creeping into my brain, ruining what should have been a beautiful day. Bill could tell it bugged me, just like I could tell he was bothered, too. We didn't talk much on the way to his gym and when we got there, he directed me to the women's locker room.

"I'll wait outside for you," he said. "Just over there." He nodded toward a low railing surrounding the stretching section at the gym.

"I meant what I said. I feel better knowing you're..." I shrugged. "You know. You're on the alert, too. Although I'm sorry to get you involved in all this crap."

"I told you. If it involves you, it involves me." He gave me an encouraging smile. "It's all just temporary, Threemie. Except for us. We're not temporary."

I laughed shakily. "Good to hear." I went into the locker room, swinging my little gym bag. Yesterday I was concerned someone was smearing Bill's name. That worry paled in comparison to today's worries. Now someone had targeted my car. Sloan as good as said it. Someone watched me, picked his time, then slashed my tires. It had to be related to the murder investigation, but how? Sloan was supposed to keep my name out of it. No one was supposed to know I was involved.

I suddenly remembered the phone call I got the night before. Who was the woman and why was she calling me? How did she get my phone number? Who was spreading stories? Who wanted me to be worried? Why was somebody trying to do this?

I wasn't finding any answers in the locker room, so I quit staring into the distance and pulled on the shorts I brought. I looked skeptically at my *Eric*

*Clapton World Tour 2001* T-shirt, which I cropped off a few years ago. It sort of covered my middle. Sort of. Oh well.

I walked out of the locker room and saw Bill waiting for me, leaning against the railing. He wore loose gym shorts, a T-shirt, and sneakers. As I suspected, he had tasty-looking legs. I was a sucker for a man with long, muscular legs.

He eyed me up and down as I approached. "Hey, coach," I said.

"Uh, Threemie, your shirt isn't long enough."

I looked down at the shirt. "I'm wearing a sports bra, Bill. If my shirt rides up a bit, there's nothing to see."

"I know you're wearing a bra. I can see it."

I followed his gaze. Oops. Yes, he could. The embroidered flowers on my bra were clearly visible next to Eric Clapton's guitar logo.

"You're liable to show a bit of skin," he pointed out.

"It's a gym. People see other people in all kinds of undress. We're all adults here." We meandered to the middle of the large indoor track where various weight machines were in use.

Bill nodded to a couple of men. "Regulars," he said in explanation. "That's Eldon Schwartz out on the track, jogging. We used to work together at the plant. And there's John North over there, on the free weights."

I smiled at the gawking onlookers. "I guess they didn't expect to see you with a strange woman."

He grinned. "You might say so. Are you okay on the machines here?"

I nodded. "They're like the ones at my gym. I really want to work on my abs. I've got some fat there and nothing I do gets rid of it."

"I use these," he said, leading me to a group of three machines.

I eyed his trim body. "Looks like it works."

He adjusted the first machine for me. "Although I don't think your little jelly roll is anything to worry about," he whispered as I struggled with the contraption.

I glared at him. "Jelly roll?"

He smiled. "I think it's sweet. Like you."

I redoubled my efforts on the machine.

When we finished two rotations, Bill said, "I usually run a bit, too." He mopped at his face with his towel.

I dabbed my face with the towel from the rack and frowned at the quarter-mile track circling the weight machines. "I don't run. In case you haven't noticed, I have breasts and I don't flop 'em around." We moved to the track and started to walk.

"I did notice."

I gave him a look of mock surprise. "You did?"

He turned around and jogged a couple of steps backward. "Yes, ma'am, I surely did."

"Good. Glad you noticed." He winked then started to run, lapping me a couple of times. I did five brisk laps then went to the cool-down area where floor mats, exercise balls and a stretching bench were positioned. I grabbed one of the big exercise balls and rolled it to one corner where one of the 'regulars' was lying on a mat, stretching.

"Hey," I said, doing a few lame sit-ups.

"Hey there." He was tall and thin with big knobby hands, probably starting to cripple with arthritis. "You a friend of Bill's?"

"Yep. Mary Madison." I extended a hand.

"Eldon Schwartz. Bill and I used to work together." He looked up when another man joined us. "We all worked together."

I nodded to the solid, stocky man who introduced himself as John North. "You've known Bill a long time?" I asked, wondering how to broach the subject of a possible rape and/or abuse.

"Oh, yeah. Years." John North grinned. "He was a floor manager down at the plant. Oh, the stories I could tell." He leaned against the low wall separating the area from the track and stretched his hamstrings.

I smiled. "Please. Share."

"He was a good manager. He sure had some difficult people working for him."

"Really?" I glanced at Bill, who was jogging stoically around the track. He looked my way and frowned. I did a few leg raises, hoping to look busy. "Difficult how?"

"Oh, a few old-timers who slacked off now and again." He grinned. "And there were a couple of rough layoffs."

"Rough? How?"

Eldon shot John a quelling look. "There wasn't anything to that."

"Hauling somebody shouting out of the plant is sort of noticeable," John said. "Calling security is something, I'd say."

"Security?" I looked at the track where Bill was rounding the bend, going out of sight. "Really?"

John looked satisfied at the little bombshell he'd dropped and decided to elaborate on it. "Yep. Tim McIntyre swore he'd get even with Bill if it was the last thing he did."

Chapter 9

I was so relieved I almost fell off the bouncy ball. It was all just a vendetta. There wasn't a damn thing to those stories. It wasn't until my worries vanished I realized how heavy they'd been. Now I had an answer.

I could trust Bill.

"This guy threatened Bill?" I asked, my voice as wobbly as my balance.

"Yep. In front of most of the shift. Hell, everybody knew it wasn't Bill's decision. If Tim was going to get pissed off at somebody, it should be the union. They hashed out the deals of each layoff with upper management. People in Bill's position were the ones who had to do the dirty work."

"How many people did he manage?"

The two men exchanged a considering look. "I don't know—maybe fifty people?" Eldon nodded. "Yeah, about that."

"Holy crap." I tipped over, the ball upending me. I was still sprawled on the floor when Bill walked over to join us.

"Hey, guys. How's it going?"

I kicked free of the treacherous exercise ball.

"John and Eldon were just telling me about your days at the factory. I didn't know you were in management."

Bill leaned both hands on the low wall separating the cool-down area from the track and stretched one leg behind him. "Lower-level management. Nothing earth-shaking."

"I ran into Tim McIntyre the other day," Eldon said. He got to his feet and bent from one side to the other, doing some half-hearted stretches.

"How's he doing?" Bill asked. Eldon and John exchanged a look, and Bill said, "What?"

"Not too good," Eldon answered. "You heard about him and Darlene?"

"She always was a slut." John glanced at me. "Sorry, but it's true."

I shrugged. "I don't know the lady."

Eldon made a face. "Not much of a lady. And it wasn't much of a marriage. They got divorced. She took up with Sammy Johnson."

I remembered Tim's litany of woe at the Coping Class the other night. He hadn't mentioned she'd left him for someone else. How it must have hurt on top of everything else. I wondered fleetingly if she'd run around on him before he got laid off. That would be another item in his Bitch List.

Bill dabbed at the sweat on his face with the towel I handed him. "I hadn't heard. It must have been tough, coming right after the layoff."

Eldon snorted. "He was lucky he wasn't laid off sooner. You did what you could for him, Bill. You kept him on long after he should have been gone."

"At least he got the severance package and the benefits," John added.

"He didn't look good," Eldon said.

John nodded agreement. "He looked like shit. Thin, pale, and he lost a lot of hair."

I thought of the man I saw in Coping Class.

*Looked bad is an understatement,* I thought. *Try looked like he was dying.*

"Where's he working now?" Bill asked.

"He's not," Eldon said with a shrug. "Never got a job."

"It's been almost three years." Bill shifted, stretching his calf muscles. I saw the tight line of his jaw and the angry look in his eyes. "He must have found something."

"Nope." John glanced at Eldon. "Maybe he's waiting for his pension to kick in."

"Yeah, he should be close," Eldon said.

"The other ones got jobs," John pointed out. "Bucky's working up at the Ford plant, Maxine is working over at Rosemount and a couple of the others are working in the Cities."

"Tim always kept to himself. Hard to tell if he even looked for a job." Eldon hopped off the bench. "Gotta go. We always have Sunday dinner with the kids. Nice to meet you, Miss Madison."

"It was nice to meet you."

He smiled, his homely face transformed into near-handsomeness. "Good to talk to you, Bill. See you next week."

"Hmm." Bill stared thoughtfully at the floor and didn't look up as Eldon, then John left the cool-down area.

"Problem?" I asked.

He looked at me, startled. "Sorry. I was thinking."

"About that guy?" I was pleased I finally had a chance to talk with him about Tim, albeit circuitously. I couldn't reveal anything Tim told me in confidence, but maybe I could get Bill's side of the story, at least.

Bill sat down on the now-vacant exercise bench. "Yeah. I had to do some layoffs a few years ago."

"It happens. It's not your fault."

"Maybe not but..." Bill ran a hand through his hair, tousling the short, sweaty strands so they stood up in spikes. "Tim took it hard. He thought he should've been promoted years before. I suppose he thought he had a job for life."

I snorted. "Nobody's got a job for life anymore."

"Yeah, but knowing that didn't help. I felt sorry for him. He was so surprised."

Bill's slumped shoulders, despondent look, and the sad tone in his voice told me how that day still haunted him. I struggled to find something to banish his blues. "It wasn't your fault, Bill." I started ambling toward the locker room. "Ready to go? I want to check out your workshop. Maybe do some puttering."

He smiled but it didn't quite reach his eyes. "Sure. Let's get on the road."

"See you in a few minutes." I went into the ladies' locker room, mentally cursing Tim McIntyre.

When we emerged from the gym, the sun was shining brightly and the mossy, moist smell in the air had none of winter's dry chill. My spirits lifted as I drove through the melting slush of the streets.

"I was thinking we'd just have snacks for lunch. I bought some apples, good bread, and cheese. Would that be okay?" Bill grinned at me, his earlier despondency dispelled. "I want to save room for your soup."

"Sounds like a plan." I turned on the CD player and Bruce Springsteen started to sing. "Let's enjoy our Sunday off."

"I'm retired, remember? I don't worry about stuff like weekends and weekdays anymore."

"Well, I do. I plan to enjoy my day off."

He put a hand on mine where it rested on the gearshift. "Thanks for spending it with me."

I wiggled my fingers under his. "My pleasure."

When we got to his house I settled on the couch

in the workshop, Mr. Magoo ensconced precariously on the cushion back above me. I stretched out and opened my first gardening magazine. Bill stood at one of the workbenches, humming along with the Beatles CD he'd put on as he updated the photo journal he was keeping on the Mustang's restoration.

"Hey, it's time to think about my next project. Would you like to work on a car?"

I looked up at him over my magazine. He was leaning on the workbench, smiling at me. "That could be interesting," I said thoughtfully. "I'm not sure what I could do, though."

"Just searching the Internet for me would be a help."

I nodded. "Easily done."

*Abbey Road* wrapped up on the CD player and Neil Young's *Harvest Moon* slid in and took the Beatles' place. I alternately read, nibbled on some food, or glanced at Bill as time passed. What a great guy. I knew him for less than a week but felt like it was a lifetime. But there was so much more to learn. I eyed him speculatively. I wanted him in bed. Was I pushing it? Rushing him? Rushing me? It had been a long time since I was with a man. What if my less-than-svelte body turned him off? What if he didn't find me attractive?

The warm sunlight filtering through the windows, combined with Neil Young's soothing lyrics, soon had me nodding off. I didn't wake until Bill walked across the workshop to sit on the edge of the couch. "What time is it?" I asked around a yawn.

"Almost five o'clock." He eased onto the couch as I scooted over, turning to face him.

"Almost time for dinner. Almost." I tugged him to me. "Let's putter."

"If you insist."

I twined my arms around his neck. "I do." Our

lips met. I felt as though someone had plunged me into a vat of warm liquid. A fire ignited in my belly and spread outward. Bill's leg edged between mine, his hard thigh pressing into my center. When his hands slid under my shirt I moaned. His fingers toyed with the hooks on my bra and I moved to give him more room. He started to pull away but I pressed against him. He rightly took that for permission and fumbled with the small hooks, soon freeing my breasts. I pulled away and he unbuttoned my shirt then tugged up the sleeveless turtleneck underneath. I flattened myself on the couch, mentally urging him to hurry, urging him to touch, taste, and feel.

Bill ran a hand up my side, capturing my breast then he kissed his way up, glancing up at me as he took my left nipple in his mouth and began a gentle suckling that soon had me gasping. I wiggled, rubbing against his thigh.

He shifted his weight and suddenly was on top, his weight gently pressing me into the couch. I felt his erection as he did so, hard and insistent. He propped himself up on his arms and looked into my eyes. "You're making me crazy, Mary Margaret Madison." He kissed me, then resumed suckling at one breast, small nips and bites making me arch with pleasure.

Years, fears, insecurities fell away. I was riding a tide of desire. He smelled fabulous: sweat, man, *Bill*. He felt marvelous: hard, smooth, rough, hairy, *Bill*. I nibbled on his neck and pressed against him, angling just right so his delicious hardness was pressed solidly right where I wanted it. How long had it been since I felt a man like this? How long had it been since these kinds of feelings made me want to throw all caution away and just *experience*? I wanted it all, I wanted sex and love and emotion. I wanted to feel him—feel him *inside*.

From a dim distance, I heard an insistent ringing sound. Bill made a disgusted noise against my breast. "Let the machine pick up," he mumbled, pulling me against him.

I gasped, all breath sucked out of me by his hard body and equally hard lips on mine. He was devouring me, his hands kneading and touching and exploring, his body moving—

"Bill, if you're there, I'd appreciate it if you'd pick up. This is Emil, from the bank. It's sort of important."

The voice paused. Bill went quiet as the words penetrated. He looked up, his eyes glazed and unseeing.

"Okay, well, listen—can you call me at home as soon as possible? Something's happened and I think we—"

"Damn," Bill breathed.

"Answer it," I said, seeing reason return to his eyes.

He looked at me desperately then flailed out with one hand and grabbed the phone from its charging cradle. "Emil. I'm here." He shifted his weight but kept me securely trapped by his legs. The banker's voice echoed through the answering machine.

"Hey, Bill, glad I caught you at home. Listen, the credit card people just called me. Someone tried to use your credit card on a phone order to Land's End. It was for $400 and the credit card company called me to verify. You didn't place an order, did you? I told them about the computer purchases, which is why they called me. We weren't expecting any other major purchases this weekend."

Bill slowly rolled away from me. "No, I didn't use it. When was it done?"

"Just an hour or two ago. The Land's End people typed in the credit card number. That bounced it to the company. They called me to verify while the purchaser was put on hold. He must have gotten wind something was up, because by the time the credit card company got back with the Land's End person, the buyer hung up." Emil blew out an exasperated breath. "If we'd acted a bit faster, we might have gotten a trace. But the ID only stays on the machine for a minute or two, and they were on hold a lot longer."

Bill swung his legs to the floor and sat up. Behind him, I fumbled with my bra. "So someone's gotten my credit card numbers?"

My fingers stilled, then I re-snapped my bra and settled my shirt. I remembered our visit to the bank and Bill's 'quarterback'—and the young woman who'd given Bill such a longing look. Combine the identity fraud with the notes, those phone calls, and my slashed car tires...what was going on? I sat up on the couch next to Bill, putting a consoling arm around his shoulders. His smile looked forced, not real.

"It's okay. I've got all your credit card numbers and your social security number on a special 'do not use' list. No one can apply for a new card, use your cards, or access your accounts. You'll need to come into the bank tomorrow and we'll make this all official. I'll have to get your signature on file again, just to be on the safe side."

Bill looked down, suddenly aware of me leaning against him, an arm around his waist. "Sure. We'll handle it tomorrow."

"Come late in the morning. I've got meetings until eleven and we'll handle it after that."

"Will do," Bill promised. "Thanks for keeping an eye on things for me."

"One of the benefits of a small town bank," Emil said with a laugh. "Sorry to interrupt your Sunday afternoon."

Bill smiled wryly at me. "It happens." He hung up the phone. "Sorry."

I nodded against his shoulder. "I thought it was all taken care of."

"I did, too." He leaned back onto the couch cushions, taking me with him. I tucked my legs under me and snuggled against his side. "Sorry I interrupted our mood."

"I get the feeling we've got a few more Sundays ahead of us. If you'd like, that is."

"Oh, yeah. I'd like."

My stomach rumbled and we both laughed. "Time for dinner," I said, starting to my feet. He pulled me back to tumble onto his lap.

"Threemie, I—" He wrapped his arms around me and said haltingly, "I think this thing with us is—I don't know, I think it's important. Maybe—"

I kissed him quickly when he stalled. "Me, too." Then his stomach rumbled. Laughing, we broke apart and left the workshop, leaving the door open for Magoo to go back into the house at his leisure.

It was dark by the time we got to my house. I was looking forward to a relaxing night of food and man when the Crisis Cell thumped on my waist. "Damn." I smiled apologetically at Bill. "I have to answer this. It's the counseling thing I told you about."

"No problem." He went to my TV and inspected the DVD player below it. "I'll make sure I know how to manage our evening's entertainment." He flourished the copy of *Last of the Mohicans* he'd brought and winked. "A great film with a combination of all kinds of action."

I laughed. "No kidding. I remember a couple of scenes..."

"No fair giving away the plot."

I smiled and moved down the hallway to the den where I could take the call in privacy. "Hello, I'm here," I said into the phone as I got comfy on the futon.

"At first I thought it was coincidence," a man said. "I've been thinking about Bill Manion for the last month and there he was, as big as life, going into the library. Then I realized it was like a sign from God."

"Tim?" I asked cautiously. I leaned forward and nudged the door closed with my foot. "What are you talking about?"

Tim snorted bitterly. "Big as life. Right. Pity I can't say the same about myself. Three years ago, Bill Manion gave me the pink slip. Now look where I am. Living in a crummy apartment, spending my days going to chemo."

"Bill didn't cause your cancer," I said softly. "He didn't cause your divorce."

"A sign from God," Tim continued, his words slurred. "That son of a bitch is responsible for everything that happened. Shouldn't life balance? Shouldn't there be some kind of repayment for what he's done to me? Don't I deserve something for it all?"

"Tim, listen to me. Are you drinking? You need to—"

"Hell, yes, I'm drinking. I know I'm not supposed to. I know how it works with the drugs, but booze is the only thing that helps with the pain. Listen, I can do whatever I want. I only have a few months left, no matter what the doctors say. Even if I get arrested, what would they do? Convict me and throw away the key? I'm dying. I've lost Darlene, I've lost the house, I've lost my job, I've lost my health..."

Good Lord, he was on a juggernaut of self pity and I couldn't stop him. Rational conversation wasn't what he was looking for. He wanted sympathy. I decided to try a different tack. "But will hurting someone else make you feel better? Think about it, Tim."

There was a long pause and I wondered if I penetrated his fog of misery. "You don't understand, do you? This is fun."

"What?" Of all the things he could have said, this wasn't what I expected.

"I'm making these last few months really count for something. I'm going to balance the scales. I was just sort of going through the motions before I saw him the other day. I almost forgot about him. But when I saw him go into the library and use the computers, I knew there had to be a reason. I knew there had to be a balance."

Good Lord. He'd been following Bill these last few days. Was that stalking? I was hazy on the legal ramifications, but if I told anyone, Tim could probably be arrested.

But I couldn't tell anyone. This was all confidential. I almost swore out loud.

Unmindful of my moral dilemma, Tim continued, his voice alternately loud then fading away. "Hell, it's been fun to figure out how to hurt him. It's almost like working again. I've got a purpose in life. I've got a reason to get out of bed in the morning." He coughed harshly and I instinctively drew away from the phone. When he resumed, his voice faded. "...new routines. Four years ago, I was in Florida on my two-week vacation, sitting on...watching Darlene in her bikini while she swam and... She and I went back to the hotel and had non-stop sex, then we'd go back to the beach the next day and do it...Now I can't even remember when the last time was I had sex."

"Listen to me. This isn't the kind of purpose you want in your life. This isn't—"

"You and Bill look like you're screwing. Or else you're close to it."

"What? What do you mean? Have you seen us

together? What—"

"I can't believe you sat in his truck and let him paw you, after what I told you. Who was the other guy who showed up? Was he a cop? I know most cops in town. Why did you call him?"

I almost dropped the phone. He was stalking us. He *was* following us.

"That's the worst part of being unemployed. You don't feel useful anymore. You've got to find a way to take up time. The unemployment counselor told me to volunteer or take part-time work to structure my day like a job, but it's not the same. It didn't have the same feeling of worth you get when you're employed."

I looked up as the door opened. Bill peeked inside. "Everything okay?" he asked softly.

I couldn't say anything. Anything said on the Crisis Cell was said in confidence unless it directly threatened someone's life. "Fine," I whispered.

"...years of interviews, applications, and resume-sending got me...Almost thirty interviews and none of them panned out. I'm over-qualified for...jobs and no employer wants to bring in a senior man at a junior man's pay. Of course, once I got the cancer..."

"Can I help?" Bill asked.

I shook my head. "I'm sorry. It's private." Who could I tell? What could I tell?

"...I lost my wife, family and home. Oh, not just because of the cancer, but because of everything. Because of Bill Manion."

I glared at Bill, who hadn't left. "I need to deal with this," I snapped.

He nodded and left, closing the door behind him. "Tim, listen to me," I said urgently. "You have to take it easy. You can't blame Bill Manion for everything that happened to you."

"I'm having too much fun to stop now. Too much fun. I've got a few more things planned for Bill. You don't want to get in my way."

"What do you mean, you've got a few more things planned? Tim, you need to be careful. You could get in serious trouble—"

"If you're smart, you'll stay away from him. You'll see."

The phone went dead in my hand.

## Chapter 10

I emerged from the den, shaking. How could I warn Bill but not reveal what I just heard? I had to maintain the confidentiality of the Crisis Cell. That was essential. But I also had to warn Bill. What to do?

Bill was sitting in the living room, petting Major Muffin. "Everything okay?" he asked.

I shook my head. "It's...complicated. I'm sorry I can't talk about it. It's all work related and it's confidential." My landline phone rang, startling me so much I almost fumbled the Crisis Cell, trying to get it into my waistband holder. I picked up the phone. "Hello?"

"Are you stupid or what?"

I looked at Bill. "It's her."

"Who?"

"The girl who called me before." I suddenly realized I hadn't told Bill about the previous phone call. I held the phone away from my ear so Bill could share the receiver. "She called last night."

"Ask him about Patty sometime. Ask him how he left her in the lurch when she was pregnant." The spiteful voice was stumbling over the words in her hurry to spit them out.

Bill's eyes widened. I put the phone back to my ear and said, "You're crazy! Bill's the nicest guy I've ever met! How do you know anything about him? What—"

"Ask him about why he dumped Patty. Better yet, ask her, she'll talk to you. Make sure you talk to Crystal or Christine. Crystal had to get away from him because he hurt her. He—"

Bill grabbed the phone out of my hand. "Who is this? Why are you doing this?"

"You don't deserve happiness after what you've done to the women in your life." The woman's voice echoed tinnily out of the phone. "You've never been faithful to a woman since I've known you. You don't deserve another chance!"

"Who are—" Bill stared down at the now-silent phone in his hand. He looked at me. "What the hell was that all about?"

I was shaking. "She called last night."

Bill slammed the phone back into its charging cradle. "What?"

I nodded. "She called last night. Right before you called."

"Why didn't you tell me? Was that why you sounded so scared last night when I called?" He paced in front of the couch, alternately glaring at me then at the phone.

I avoided his gaze. "I don't know."

He stopped and stared at me. "I know why. You don't trust me."

I took a step away from him. He looked like he wanted to shake me. Instead he took a deep, steadying breath, jamming his hands in his pockets as though stopping himself. "Patty and I—After we broke up she got married right away and had a kid. But it's not my kid. And Crystal—" He flushed. "I told you about it. That didn't work out."

"What do you mean?"

He ran a hand through his hair, looking anywhere but at me. "I couldn't please Crystal or Christine." He turned away, going into the kitchen. "They just..."

I followed him, bewildered. "What?" I stopped when the phone rang again. "Damn, what's the deal? I never get this many phone calls." I snatched up the phone, glancing into the kitchen where Bill was standing, staring out the window. "What?" I snapped into the phone.

"And a good evening to you, too," Detective Sloan said. "Glad to see you're safe at home, all snug and warm."

"What do you want? I'm busy."

"Ah. The gentleman caller still there?" He hurried on before I could answer. "I just wanted to make sure you were at home. The squad car will be making regular sweeps through your neighborhood. If you have any problems, you give me a call."

"I'll be fine."

"I'm sure you will be. But I'm just doing my civic duty."

"Thanks." I slammed down the phone, unable to cope with a Mr. Grumpy who, for some inexplicable reason, wasn't grumpy. I hurried into the kitchen where Bill was putting on his jacket.

"I need to think about all of this. I don't understand why somebody's doing this to me." He avoided looking at me, his face red. "I never hurt anybody. I never did anything somebody didn't want. I know how it looked but—Can you believe me?"

"What?" I stepped back a pace, not sure what I was hearing.

"I'll call you tomorrow. I have to go to the bank but I'll call you afterwards."

"Bill, I don't understand." I took a cautious step toward him.

"I'll call you." He fled, almost running for his truck.

I heard his truck start and looked out the kitchen window. He backed out of the drive then shot off up the street without a glance back. I stared at the tire tracks in the snow then walked back into the living room. "I don't understand."

I snatched up my car keys from the end table and went outside, moving Stella from its spot at the curb to the garage. Good thing I made sure he had an easy out. Why did he run away? What did the phone call mean? I closed the garage then went into the house, locking all doors behind me. Sgt. Snuggle, annoyed at the preemptive male visitor who'd invaded her space, stalked out of her hiding spot and glared at me. I glared back and went into the living room to flop on the couch.

What the hell was happening? I shot to my feet, unable to sit still, and started to pace. When the phone rang, I jumped so high I stumbled as I grabbed the receiver. "What?"

"Stupid bitch." I heard a low, malicious laugh, then a dial tone.

"Shit." I slammed the phone down but it rang again almost immediately.

"Bitch. I'm glad he left." Dial tone.

"Damn." Was someone watching me? I turned off the light and sidled around the corner to the kitchen, turning off the light there, too.

The phone rang again. I stumbled through the darkness and started to reach for it, but stopped when I saw lights in the distance, in my back yard.

Oh, shit. Somebody was out there. Where to go? I briefly considered getting into Stella and driving away, but if someone was watching me, they might follow. The bedroom had a good view of the back yard. I would check that light first. I bolted, clutching the telephone that rang as I dashed down the hall. I bounced off the door frame as the phone rang again.

"If you're not careful—"

"Leave me alone," I snapped, then broke the connection. I inched through the bedroom, feeling like a faux James Bond as I stealthily approached the window. I peeked up and over the sill.

A light was bobbing in the park beyond my yard and it was heading my way.

The phone rang again. "Listen, you bitch, leave me alone," I said before the caller could fit in a word.

There was a pause. "Sorry? Did I interrupt something?"

I almost wept with relief at hearing Sloan's voice.

"You sounded upset earlier, so I figured I'd call back. If there's a problem, I can swing by. You're not far from my house, and—"

"Detective Sloan?" I whispered.

"What's wrong? Are you whispering? Am I interrupting something? Oh, shit. Your boyfriend's still there, isn't he? I didn't interrupt anything, did I?"

"Someone's outside."

I could imagine his jaw dropping. "What do you mean?"

My voice was hoarse and wobbly. "I saw lights in the park across the way."

"Where are you?"

"I'm hiding in the bedroom. I wasn't sure what to do."

"You should have called me."

"Excuse me, but I don't have your phone number tattooed on my arm," I shot back. "It's on your card, which is in my wallet which is in my purse which is in the living room."

"I'll have a squad car check it. Hold on, I'm using my cell phone to call it in."

"But—" I heard him talking in a low voice but I didn't catch the words. Then he came back on the line.

"The squad is going to the park. They'll drive by your place, too. If you want them to stop, turn on all your lights, okay? I'll be there in a minute. Stay put."

I hated to admit it, but it was just what I wanted to hear. "I'll be here." I hung up the phone then turned off the ringer so it wouldn't surprise the pee out of me if it rang. A few seconds later I heard the answering machine click on in the living room. The bitter female voice said something. I didn't need to hear the words to know it was vicious.

I sagged against the wall, staring at the clock and willing the minutes to pass. They did, but agonizingly slowly. After four minutes and two more phone calls, I ventured a look outside again. The lights were still wobbling around.

Muffin sauntered into the room, unsurprised to see me crouching below the window. "Hey, Major," I whispered.

He flopped down on the floor next to me and stretched. Reassured by his calmness, I stood up and peeked out the window, checking the lights in the distance. Muffin jumped up on the trunk near the window and put both paws on the sill. "Get down," I whispered, tugging on him. He responded by trying to get upon the sill, falling off, and stalking out of the room, tail twitching. "Idiot."

The answering machine in the living room clicked on again. "Mary? Mary, pick up."

It was Sloan. I answered cautiously. "What?"

"I'm on the road," Sloan said. "What's happening? Has someone been calling you?"

All the stress of the day started to accumulate. I sniffled. "I—it's—I—"

"Mary, what happened?"

He sounded concerned and curious as all hell. Words started to tumble out. I hoped he could parse what I was saying. When I finally ground to a halt, he said, "So, a guy has told you Manion's no good and a woman called. Manion says yeah, he did date those women. What's the problem?"

Phrased that way, it did sound odd. Luckily I had a diversion. "Oh. The police are there. I can see them. There're big flashlights across the way there."

"Good." There was a pause. "Mary?"

"Well, I don't know and that's the problem. He acted so odd. He just ran out of here. We were...you know...on the couch then he just ran out of here. What's it mean?" I peered some more. "The flashlights are moving around."

"If it's any consolation, I ran a check on Manion. He came back clean. No arrests, no run-ins with the law. I'm here."

"You did what?" Disbelief warred with relief. Relief won. I sagged back again, glad to know the rumors were unfounded. I heard a car in my front drive and my stomach clenched. "You're where? You did what? You ran a background check on him?"

"I'm here, at your house. I'm pulling in the driveway. Open the door."

I shot to my feet, stalked to the front door and flung it open as Marcus Sloan got out of his car. His cell phone was still in his hand.

"I checked him out. I wanted to know who was messing with my witness."

"He's not...messing! I mean, really, how could you—"

His cell phone rang. "Hang on."

"I will not! I will not—" I jammed my feet into my clogs and went out to confront Sloan, who was just closing his phone. "Who was that?"

"The squad car, checking in. They found tracks but nobody was there. Come on, let's go in your house." He steered me through the front door, closing it firmly behind him. "So what's the problem? I thought you and he were having a nice, quiet night at home tonight." He sniffed. "Smells good."

"I'll give you some to take home." I went into the kitchen and turned on the lights. "Bill didn't stay long enough to eat."

Sloan watched as I jerked open a drawer and pulled out a Tupperware container. "Do you trust him?"

"That's not the point!"

"Of course it is."

I glared at him.

"At some point, you go with your instincts. You either believe a nasty voice on the phone or you believe the guy you've been necking with."

"We weren't—" I stopped and he grinned. "Okay, we were." I reached for the lid to the crockpot but dropped it as soon as I touched it, the heat searing up through my fingers. "Damn!" I shouted, jumping back as the glass exploded over the floor. "This is the cap to a lousy day." I knelt down to pick up the bigger shards but Sloan beat me to it.

"Hey, hey, come on, now. Relax." He pushed my hands aside. "You go chill and I'll deal with this."

I sat down suddenly on the floor, overwhelmed. "I can't chill until I find out what's going on." I wiped at the tears starting to ooze down my cheeks.

"Oh, man, don't cry. Come on, we'll figure out what's going on." He sat back on his heels and regarded me. "I'll go talk to Manion, see what's happening, okay? Tomorrow."

I shook my head, not trusting myself to speak.

"Okay, okay. Tonight."

I shook my head again. "I want to go with you."

"He won't talk if you're with me."

"I need to know."

"No way."

I stared at him, tears rolling down my face.

\*\*\*\*

Twenty minutes later, we pulled into Bill's driveway. The house was dark but lights blazed in the workshop. "That's the shop," I whispered from the back seat of Sloan's car. "He's there."

"Stay back there and don't move," Sloan commanded. "Don't make a peep. I'll come back and tell you what he said."

He got out of the car. I couldn't help myself. "Peep."

Sloan glared down at me then strode to the workshop door, rapping sharply on it. I peeked over the front seat, peering between the uprights on the headrest of the front passenger seat. I saw the door open and Bill looked out. "Detective Sloan? What are you doing here? Is everything okay?"

"Can I come in? I want to talk to you about Mary Madison."

Bill's face paled so rapidly I was afraid he'd pass out. "Is she okay? What happened?"

Sloan pushed past him.

I agonized for a couple of seconds, then got out of the car and scurried to the window on the side of the shop. A small exhaust fan took the place of a lower quarter of the glass and even though it was covered by a metal plate, I could still hear voices. I hunkered down to listen.

"What's happened with Mary? Is she okay?"

"You tell me," Sloan said. "Why'd you run out on her?"

I ventured a look through the window. As quickly as Bill's face paled, it flooded with color. "What?"

"She told me about the phone call. She was scared and it all came out."

"Why was she scared?" Bill picked up a towel from a workbench and started scrubbing his already clean hands.

"Someone was in the park behind her house."

"What?" Bill dropped the towel and strode toward Sloan. "Why aren't you there? Hell, why aren't *I* there? I should be watching out for her. What if—"

"The patrol checked it out. Whoever was there is gone now. Look, just for my own curiosity, why'd you run out on her? She's upset. She doesn't know what to think."

"It's none of your business." Bill turned away.

"She's my witness. She's upset because of you. It's my business."

Bill tugged on the towel. "She's been getting these phone calls."

"Yeah. She told me."

"Well, shit." Bill jammed his hands deep into his jeans pockets.

"So what's the deal? You dated those women, right? I mean, big deal." Sloan shrugged. "You dated."

"Yeah." The word was long and drawn out. "But...oh, hell. Crystal was..." Bill looked desperate. "She was crazy. Crazy about sex."

Sloan and I both straightened in surprise. "And that was a problem?"

"No kidding," I whispered.

"I mean..." Bill looked around, like he was looking for words. "She wanted to try everything." He looked intently at Sloan. "Everything."

"Every..." Sloan's voice trailed away. "Whoa. You mean like...Everything? Multiple partners and...?"

"And I just...couldn't." Bill's face flooded with color as he turned away, examining a notebook on the workbench. "Not all the time. You know."

"You couldn't..." Sloan cleared his throat then his face got red, too.

I blinked in surprise. Was I hearing what I

thought I was hearing?

Sloan apparently heard the same thing I did. "It happens to everybody now and then. It happens all the time." He shrugged, looking anywhere but at Bill.

Bill nodded. "But then the next woman...Christine. She...I sometimes..."

Now Sloan turned away to studiously examine the Mustang. "Well, shit. What about since then?"

"That's just it. There hasn't been anybody. Not until Threemie."

"What is it with this 'Threemie' thing?" Sloan asked. "No, forget it, it's not important. So what you're saying is, you're worried this...thing...this occasional...thing might be happening?"

I wanted to throw my hands in the air and scream. Impotence? I know it had been a long time since I was with a man, but there were a few things a girl remembered and the feeling of an erect penis was one of them. I was pretty damn sure Bill's problem wasn't impotence. Only clothing had separated us and if I had my way, we would have dispensed with it.

Impotence?

"Well, I don't think so," Bill confessed, his face still red. "I mean, when I'm with her I sure don't have a problem but who knows when we finally get into bed and..." He shrugged. "I can't talk to her about it! What do I say—*oh, by the way, those stories are right, Crystal did like it rough but sometimes I just couldn't accommodate her?*" Bill gave a brief, brittle laugh.

Sloan considered it. "It happens to every man now and again. She'll understand. Just tell her you're...you know, you're worried." Bill shot him a disgusted look. "Yeah, yeah. I know. That's lame. You're right."

They stood in thoughtful silence, Sloan by the

Mustang and Bill by the workbench. Magoo snored in masculine sympathy from the couch, paws twitching. "Well, if you care about her, you've got to take the chance," Sloan finally said. "But if she's just a one-nighter then who cares? Don't bother."

Bill glared at him. "She's more than a one-nighter."

"Then you've got to try it. You said you—when you and she—hell, just try it. I'm betting it'll be fine. Those phone calls didn't imply..."

Bill shook his head. "No. From what I heard, they accused me of hurting women."

Sloan snorted. "So they're going on rumor. Small towns; they're the worst. Someone probably got drunk and starting dropping hints."

"Probably Crystal. She's the type who'd do something like that."

"There you are. I'm the last person in the world to be giving romantic advice, but it seems to me Mary Madison is a woman worth taking a chance for."

"Yeah," Bill said slowly. "I'm asking her to trust me. I guess I need to do the same. I need to trust her."

"Yeah." Sloan moved away from the car and stuck his hands in the pockets of his jeans again. I could tell from his posture his romantic intervention had run its course. The cop was back. "Listen, I'm worried about the park thing tonight. I'm going to have a squad follow her to work tomorrow. Are you two going to be together tomorrow night?"

Bill nodded. "I hope so."

"Keep me in the loop. I don't want her left alone."

Bill smiled. "I can do it. I'm retired."

"Lucky guy." Sloan looked around the shop. "Nice place."

Bill glanced at the couch where he and I had

lounged. "Yeah, it is."

I saw Sloan start to head toward the exit and I whirled, making a dash for the car. I flung myself into the back seat, managing to close the door just as the shop door closed behind Sloan.

"Get an earful?" he asked as he slid into the driver's seat.

"I beg your pardon? Turn up the heat, would you? It's cold in here."

He glanced at me in the rear view mirror. "You didn't sneak up there to listen in?"

"Please. I'm not good at spy business. With my luck I'd fall over something and make so much noise you'd hear me. So tell me what he said."

"Will you trust me if I say it's nothing to do with you?"

"No."

"I figured you'd say that." He drove out of Bill's neighborhood, obviously deep in thought. "Listen, it's a guy thing. Is that enough for you?"

"No. What kind of guy thing?"

He shook his head. "Let me think about it, okay? It's confidential."

I subsided back on the seat. "There's too damn much confidential crap flying around," I muttered.

"No shit," he agreed.

## Chapter 11

I spent the night sleeping with a 9-iron next to me in bed. A hard piece of metal wasn't as much fun as the hard man I hoped to have.

The thought gave me pause when I woke up in the morning, Major Muffin pushing against my legs and my nine-iron poking me in the boob. Was I truly willing to have Bill in my bed? Was I really ready to take that kind of chance? I'd only known the guy a few days. Granted, he was a great kisser and I had hopes he'd be an equally great lover, but should I really throw caution to the winds?

Maybe I wouldn't get the chance. I decided to worry about it when and if the time came.

Promptly at nine in the morning I turned off the Crisis Cell, happy to have done with it. The damn phone had brought me nothing but trouble. When I got to the office I found a message on my phone from Mark, Billy's brother, at the hospital. *"He's doing okay, but he's fading. I'll keep you in the loop, Threemie, but...it looks close. All the relatives were in town last weekend. I think it's what he was waiting for. He just wanted to say good-bye. I'll call you later."*

I felt a stab of grief at the thought of Billy, wasting away, his whooping laugh and raucous sense of humor silenced forever. I blinked back tears and opened up my on-screen calendar, only to find I was facing three hours of morning meetings, an afternoon of writing and research, and an evening of—

What? What could I look forward to? Would Bill come back? If he didn't come back, I didn't have a chance to prove to him the impotence thing was all a bunch of crap. At least, I thought it would be a bunch of crap.

Why was it all so complicated?

I doodled on my notepad during my second meeting, drawing little hearts tragically ruptured in two. Rajid Bashanti, one of the engineers on the project, peered over my arm at the hearts and made a 'tsk' noise. I jerked the notepad away from his inquisitive eyes.

I stifled a yawn but choked on it when I saw Kate gesturing outside the conference room door. I closed my eyes, praying for strength then picked up my notepad and got out of the room. One look at Kate's face told me everything.

"It was Mark. He just called."

"I'll be at the hospital if anybody needs me," I said, snatching up my jacket and purse. "I'll probably be gone tomorrow."

Kate nodded, her thin face pinched. "Call me if you can." She hugged me then stumbled away, brushing at her tears.

I took a deep breath and steeled myself for a last hospital visit.

My cell phone rang as I got out of Stella on the fifth floor of the parking garage near the hospital. "It's Threemie," I said, tugging my purse out of the car.

"What is it with that Threemie thing?"

I threw back my head and stared at the ceiling of the parking garage, praying for strength. "Detective Sloan." I jerked the purse and it sprang free. I stumbled backwards, almost toppling. "Why are you bothering me?"

"I'm trying to be a nice guy. Give me a break."

"Why?"

"Why what?"

"Why are you trying to be a nice guy?"

There was a long pause. I hurried to the stairwell. "It might come in handy some day. Look, I thought about Manion last night and what he and I talked about. Give the guy some slack. He's worried."

"About what?"

"About you. About how you feel about him."

I paused as I tugged open the stairwell door. "Well, duh. What's to worry about? Why doesn't he just ask me?"

"What would you say?"

"None of your damn business. You're not my matchmaker."

"I feel like one. Look, this is a guy thing. He's worried about...*guy* things." Sloan put a special emphasis on the words.

"It's what?" I hurried down the stairs, wrinkling my nose at the layer of salt and cinder on the treads, obviously tracked in by patrons.

"It's a guy thing. You know—he's an *older* guy and you're a *younger* babe and he's worried about—you know—*guy* things."

"Guy..." I let my voice trail away. "Are you saying he's worried he can't—he won't be able to..."

"Yeah." Sloan blew out a big sigh. "You know—*guy* things."

I almost laughed at the sound of relief in his voice. I raced down the remainder of the stairs. "I may not be an expert, but I don't think it'll be a problem."

Sloan laughed. "Yeah, well, men don't think that way. They worry about stuff like that. All I'm saying is, when you got those calls, it brought up some unpleasant memories for him *if you know what I mean.*" He put an ominous emphasis on the final words.

"Oh. Okay." I almost laughed out loud at Sloan's careful phrasing. A guy thing, indeed.

"Yeah. So give him a break. Be nice to him."

"Why'd he tell you this?" I asked as I strolled through the catwalk.

"We're men united by a common confusion with women. Anyway, that's only part of why I called. I talked to the captain in charge of the investigation. He's getting a line-up set up. It's tricky, though, because we need a mix of street guys and cops."

I paused at the doorway to the hospital. "I have to hang up now. I'm going into the hospital. Can I call you later?"

"What for? Are you okay?"

"I'm fine. I'm visiting a friend."

"Okay, well, listen. I'll call you tonight. I'll call you or Manion."

"I may not be with him."

"You will be. Trust me. I know these things. I'll be in touch."

"Okay." I folded up the cell phone and stuffed it into my purse. I glanced at the entrance desk on the third floor outside the catwalk then stopped when I saw Bill sitting near the desk, pressing a bag of ice to his forehead. "Bill?"

He looked up. "Threemie? Why are you here?"

"Why are you here?" I sat next to him, putting a hand on his arm. "Bill, you're hurt!"

"It's just a bruise." He pulled the ice pack away and I saw the dark splotch on his pale face and the dark line of a cut, with small stitches holding it

136

closed. "I'm fine. I've just got a headache now."

"What happened?"

"Car accident. I was leaving the bank and somebody clipped me. Then another car ran right into me." He shifted his weight and winced. "I'm bruised."

"That's terrible. Are they going to admit you?"

He shook his head gingerly. "Nah. Somebody checked me over in the emergency room and now I'm waiting for papers or something. I'll call a cab and go home. The truck's in bad shape."

"I'll drive you." Then I remembered. "Oh. I can't. It's Billy."

He put a hand on mine where it rested on his arm. "Is he...?" I nodded, tears starting. "Do you want me to go with you?"

"I can't ask you to do that." I was amazed at the rush of relief and gratitude I felt at his offer. "You're hurt and you need to rest."

He stood up, tugging me to my feet. "I'd like to help."

"Thanks." I looked up as a nurse approached. "Looks like you've got your walking papers."

Bill signed the necessary forms and took the papers and a small plastic bag containing two pills. "You shouldn't be alone tonight," the nurse said. "If your headache gets any worse or if your vision starts to blur, you need to come in. Take one of those pills tonight and one tomorrow if you need it. They do cause drowsiness, though, so be careful."

I took the papers from Bill and glanced through them. "Not a problem," I said. "I'll keep an eye on him."

Bill smiled tiredly. "We'll keep an eye on each other." He put an arm round my shoulders and I felt him sag against me. "Let's go."

The ICU was two floors up. I paused by the stairwell door but I could feel Bill's exhaustion next to me. I gamely punched the elevator button and we rode upward for the mercifully short ride.

We went into the room where Mark and Janine, his wife, were sitting. Billy was resting, his face pallid and so thin. Most of the tubes and lines were gone now. Only two IVs led into his frail arm. Mark looked up as we entered. I introduced Bill, and he and Mark shook hands. Then I took a seat on Billy's right side and put my hand on his. Bill stood behind me, one hand gently squeezing my shoulder.

Billy's eyes fluttered open. They were a shadow of those vibrant gray eyes I remembered, eyes snapping with laughter and mischief. Now he looked bewildered and tired. I smiled and he smiled back, a brief tugging of the muscles. His gaze flickered to Bill. "Who's—?" he croaked.

"A friend of mine."

Bill leaned forward and put his hand over mine where it rested on Billy's thin, claw-like hand. He met Billy's ravaged eyes and some message was exchanged. Billy smiled tiredly.

"Good." He took a deep, shuddering breath. I held my breath, wondering how my poor, decimated friend managed it. "It's good my girl has someone."

Bill leaned back, putting his hands on my shoulders. "She does."

Billy's gaze wandered to the corner of the room. "I talked to Garth today," he said in a halting, rasping voice. "He's waiting for me." I nodded, unable to speak. Mark leaned forward, his hand clasping his brother's. "I can't wait to see him."

Mark nodded, his face calm. "I know." When Billy had been healthy, they'd looked remarkably alike. Now Billy was a terrible caricature of his older brother. "It's okay if you want to go," Mark said softly.

Billy moved his head, his once thick brown hair now wispy and thin. "I think I will." He took a labored, agonized breath. Mark's hand closed around Billy's, gently and firmly. I stiffened under Bill's hands. Billy's labored breathing became harsher until it seemed to fill every inch of space in the room.

Then suddenly it was very quiet.

**\*\*\*\***

The rest of the afternoon passed in a quiet fog of tears and talk. We all went to a "family lounge" where I called Kate and cried while Bill held me. Emil called Bill on his cell phone, concerned when he heard about his accident. Then the police came to talk to Bill about the accident. He went outside with them and called his insurance agent, who heard about the accident from Emil. By four in the afternoon, I was exhausted.

"Thanks for being here," Mark said as we all bundled into our coats to leave. His gaze flickered to Bill, who had an arm securely around my shoulders. "We appreciate it."

"I wish I'd known him," Bill said.

Mark looked surprised then he smiled. "I think you two would have gotten along, and not just because of the names." He kissed me on the cheek. "Cremation tomorrow, then we'll release his ashes and Garth's together on Thursday at the Arboretum, like he wanted."

I nodded. "Just let me know the time. I'll be there."

"We'll be there, if it's okay," Bill said, once again pulling me against him.

Mark nodded. "I'll call."

Bill started toward the elevators. *Only two floors,* I repeated silently to myself. *I can handle it.* I held onto him as the elevator lurched into motion. He winced at the movement and his body stiffened against mine. "Are you okay?" I asked.

"I'm just tired. And there's the headache."

"Still?" The doors opened and we moved out into

the corridor leading to the catwalk.

He nodded. "The doctor gave me some pills but he said they'd make me sleepy. I figured I'd take one tonight."

I steered him toward the elevator in the parking garage. *It's only two floors*, I told myself. *Don't think about it. It'll be fine.* I glanced up at Bill, frowning at the sight of the bruise on his forehead. He looked exhausted, his face rigid as he tried to keep his head still.

We got into the old elevator and it chugged upward. "Let's grab something to eat and take it to your place," I suggested. "You're beat, I'm beat, and we need to relax."

"You talked me into it."

I led him to my car where he folded himself into the passenger side. "Will you need to get a rental? How long will it take to fix your car?"

He leaned back against the headrest. "I'm not sure. There's a place in town where I can rent a car. I'll go there tomorrow. I talked to Del, down at the truck shop, and he said it'll be a week or so for the repairs so I'll need to rent a car."

"I can drive you over," I volunteered, steering onto the street. "Where do you want to go for supper?"

"I don't care. Let's just get some drive-through, okay?"

I glanced at him and saw the lines of pain around his jaw and the sagging weariness in his shoulders. "Sure. We'll decide about the rental later."

"Decide what?" Bill asked tiredly.

I put a gentle hand on his leg. "Don't worry. You need to rest and recuperate. We'll eat something then I'll take you home and tuck you in."

He turned his head to regard me, his eyes narrowed in pain. "Will you tuck in with me?"

I smiled. "You big old flirt. Of course."

He sighed and closed his eyes.

****

It took all of Bill's strength to slip off his coat and boots then stagger into his tiny dining room, even with my help. He forced down a few bites of hamburger, some salad, and fries then I insisted he take one of the pain pills.

"I don't need it," he protested, wincing when he glanced at the setting sun.

"Bullshit. Men always say they don't need drugs. You need it. Take it."

He took the pill from my outstretched hand and swallowed it with a sip of Pepsi. He watched me tidy up the remains of the meal. "You don't have to do that. I can do it tomorrow."

"Or I can do it tonight." I touched his bruised face gently. "You should lie down."

"Yeah." He staggered toward the living room, heading for the couch.

I put an arm around his waist. "Let's put you to bed. Rest will be the best thing for you."

"I'll just nap on the couch."

"No, you won't. I won't fit comfortably on the couch with you." I spied the staircase off the living room and aimed toward it.

"You're going to stay with me?" Bill climbed the stairs, one hand on the railing pulling him up with me on the other side, tugging him with an arm around his waist.

"Yep. Remember? The nurse said you shouldn't be left alone."

"But you've got to work."

"Hush. I'll call Kate and she'll check on my cats. I'm going to work late tomorrow, so I can sleep in." He blinked at me, trying to understand. "Come on." We paused in the small foyer at the top of the stairs. "Bedroom?"

141

Bill looked at the three doorways facing him. "Bathroom." He vanished inside.

I waited, leaning against the wall and listening for the sound of a body hitting the floor. What I heard instead was the sound of peeing. I breathed out a sigh of relief. If he could manage bodily functions, he was probably okay.

When the door fumbled open Bill winced at the overhead light.

"Which way?" I asked.

He looked at the doorway opposite and I put an arm around his waist and started steering him toward the room. When we got inside, I saw the double bed with brown bedspread and plain wood dresser. "It's not much," he mumbled, sitting on the edge of the bed.

"It's nice. Lift your arms."

"Huh?"

"Lift your arms." I tapped his arms and Bill lifted them. I whisked off his shirt, leaving his T-shirt on. "Now stand up."

"Huh?"

I tugged him to his feet and started to unbuckle his belt. "Threemie!"

"Honestly, Bill. We're grown-ups." I unbuckled his belt, unzipped his pants, and was soon tugging them down around his legs. He fell back on the bed, dizzy and disoriented. I slipped the jeans off, tossed them aside then bundled Bill under the covers before he knew what had happened. I leaned over him. "You sleep now," I whispered, kissing him on the cheek.

"I want to sleep with you," he mumbled, his eyes closing.

"You will," I promised. I left the room, looking once behind me. Bill was already asleep.

I fed Magoo then sank down onto the couch. I hadn't slept much the night before and it was catching up to me. Before I dozed off I called Kate, and we had another good cry about Billy. She didn't even quibble when I told her about Bill's car accident and that I was staying there for the night. "Just be careful, okay?" she said.

"I'm trying to be."

I ran through my mental checklist, wondering who else I needed to call. Sloan. Was he calling me or was I calling him? I couldn't remember. I yawned and considered Bill's couch. It looked comfortable.

Then I remembered his bed. It looked a lot more comfortable. I went upstairs, shucked off my clothes, pulling on a T-shirt I found in a dresser drawer before slipping into the bed. Bill was sound asleep and didn't stir except to mumble slightly as I got under the covers.

I was just dropping off to sleep when the phone rang. I picked up the extension by the side of the bed. "Bill Manion's house."

"I told you, didn't I? I knew you'd be at his house." Sloan's voice was smug and humor filled. "Hey, that's right. It's his house. How come you're answering the phone?"

I told him about Bill's car accident. "This is getting weird," Sloan said. "Tires slashed, car accident, credit card fraud. I don't get it."

"I think I do," I said sleepily. "But it's too complicated to tell you tonight. I have to think of a way to tell you confidential information without really telling you."

There was a long pause. "You'll explain it the next time I see you, right? Which reminds me, I got the line-up okayed. When's the best time for you?"

"Schedule it for tomorrow. Bill needs me tonight."

Sloan laughed. "You know, when I said to be nice, I didn't mean you had to babysit the guy."

"He's injured, for cryin' out loud. He's passed

out. I'm not going to get that lucky."

"Hey, you never know."

"Right. Call me tomorrow about the line-up. I can do it later in the afternoon."

"Sounds good. I'll have patrol keep an eye on the house. Good night, Mary."

"Good night, Detective." I managed to fumble the phone into the cradle and dropped back on the bed. As I did, Bill turned over and snuggled against me, obviously still asleep. He put out his hand and touched my breast. His fingers tightened and he massaged me gently, murmuring something as he did so.

Suddenly his eyes flew open. "Threemie?"

I touched his face. "One and the same. I borrowed a T-shirt. I hope you don't mind. I didn't want to wake up wrinkled. I fed the cat, too. He looked hungry."

"Threemie, what are you doing here?"

"You asked me to sleep with you." I kissed the tip of his nose. "Should I leave? How are you feeling?" I turned and slid my leg along his, moving sinuously up his thigh to nudge him gently in the groin. "Certain parts of you feel great, but how's the rest of you feeling?"

He tore his eyes from my face to look around the room. The hallway light was on, adding its illumination to the moonlight. "What time is it?"

"Midnight. Do you want to take another pain pill? The doctor said you could take the pills six hours apart." I slipped a hand under his T-shirt and his stomach tensed.

"Pain pill? For what? I'm fine."

"Are you sure you feel okay?" I eyed him as I ran my hand down his chest, pausing at the waistband of his shorts.

"Threemie, if I feel any better I'll die and go to heaven," he croaked. "But I wanted this to be special. I mean, I was hoping we would...well, you know. And I wanted it to be special."

"What do you mean?" I nibbled against his neck and he shivered.

"Special. You know, a nice dinner, maybe some wine, some dessert."

I laughed. "This isn't special?" I sat up and skinned off the T-shirt I was wearing then leaned over, pinning his hands to the bed. "I've got you just where I want you. And now you can answer a question I've had since I met you."

He flexed his hands upward, clasping my fingers. "What's that?"

"I want to see what's been poking me in the stomach for the last few days." I pulled the covers aside. "Show me."

He did.

Chapter 12

"You promised you'd make me breakfast," I mumbled.

Bill stirred beside me. "It's not even daylight." His hand strayed over my bare hip then up my stomach to cup my breast. "Can't you wait?"

I snuggled deeper into the pillow and deepened my breathing. "If you insist."

"Hey, I didn't mean go back to sleep." He rolled me over, laughing. I looped my arms around his neck as he nuzzled me, rasping me with his beard. "Good morning."

"How are you feeling?" I asked, touching the bruise on his forehead. The bruise on his arm the night before had spread to cover his entire right shoulder in a yellow and purple stain.

"Stiff," he said, nudging me with a stiffened appendage.

"I know just the thing to relax you." I wiggled a bit until I was underneath him.

"I'm sure you do."

"Shall I show you?"

"Please do."

Some time later, I reluctantly moved away from

him. Bill was sprawled on his back with a look of such relaxed contentment I hated to shatter the mood. "I have to get up. I do need to check in at work, at least briefly." I also had Crisis Cell duty, but I wasn't about to mention it, not after having an incendiary night of high-octane sex. Such a prosaic thing as work and responsibility seemed out of place.

Bill turned his head on the pillow, watching as I plucked up the discarded T-shirt from the bedroom floor. "Why don't you retire with me? We could spend our days making love and restoring old cars."

"That's an offer which might be hard to pass up." I skittered away from his groping hand. "But I don't have enough in my 401K to wile my days away. I still need to work."

"I could make you a kept woman."

I paused as I tugged on the T-shirt then smoothed it down. "I wouldn't do well as a kept woman. I'm too independent."

"I meant it, Threemie. We can get married." His dark eyes met and held mine.

"You hardly know me," I pointed out. "I hardly know you."

He smiled. "We could have an engagement and get to know each other."

I edged away from the bed, toward the bathroom. "We've just met." He eased out of bed, wincing. "Are you okay?"

"I've used a few muscles I haven't used in a while." He sat on the edge of the bed and stretched.

I admired the view as he did so. "Bragging or complaining?"

He laughed. "Believe me, I'm not complaining. About this engagement thing—I believe in love at first sight. When you dragged me into the garage, you sealed your fate."

"I never did. You are such a liar, Bill Irishman!" I spun around and headed for the bathroom.

Bill pounced, grabbing me from behind and sandpapering my face. "Think about it?"

I looked at him, seeing the love in those liquid blue eyes. "I will. But first I have to face the real world. And we need to get you a car."

"First we shower together. I want to get you all soapy in my bathroom. *Then* we face the real world."

I grinned. "Deal."

It was almost nine o'clock before I sat down in Bill's little dining room to enjoy the breakfast he prepared for me. I slipped on the Crisis Cell headset, hiding it under my hair and clipping the phone to my waistband. I would call Hal later on and see if he could take it for me on Thursday. I didn't want to be monitoring the phone while I went to Billy's memorial service.

Bill set a plate in front of me with a flourish. Magoo, dozing near my feet, looked up with interest. He'd followed me from the moment I came out of the bedroom, obviously having decided I was a person worth monitoring.

I looked down at the egg, three pieces of bacon, and slice of toast. "You do good work." I broke off a piece of bacon and Magoo accepted it with delicate agility, belying his age.

Bill sat down opposite me with his own plate. "You look nice, sitting there at my table."

I smiled at him. "And you'll look nice at my table, too."

"One of us will need to sell a house, won't we? Once we get married."

"As I recall, we were going to discuss it further."

He nodded, his dark eyes laughing. "I'm just pointing out if you don't have a mortgage payment, you could probably retire sooner."

I paused, fork halfway to my mouth. "Your house is paid off?"

"I'm frugal."

I wonder if he saw the mercenary gleam in my eye. Paying off my mortgage had long been a goal. In the back of my mind I had always thought, "no mortgage payment, no worries."

"Just something to consider. Not to mention the fact I'd be available to shovel the walk, mow the lawn, rake the leaves, and do a lot of the other manly stuff." He dug into his two eggs, bacon, and toast with gusto. "I worked up an appetite last night." He grinned at me. "And this morning. I need to keep up my strength."

I laughed at his smug expression. "You would be convenient to have around."

"And there's the whole evening thing," he continued.

"Evening thing?"

Bill's phone rang. "I'd better get it. The insurance people might call." He took three steps and reached around the open archway to grab the phone from the wall unit. "Bill Manion here." He paused, glancing at me with amusement. "Yeah. Hold on." He held the portable phone to me.

"Me? Who knew I was here? Oh, wait a minute. Kate." I took the phone. "It's Threemie."

"Are you going to explain that Threemie thing?" Sloan demanded.

"How'd he know I was still here?" I asked. Bill shrugged then winced. I saw and winced with him. "Does it hurt?"

"Not at all," Sloan said. "How about you?"

"I wasn't talking to you. Honestly, you're the nosiest man in the world." I nibbled my bacon. "What do you want?"

"You sound grumpy today," Sloan commented. "Didn't you sleep well last night? As I recall, you told me you were going to keep an eye on Manion. How's he doing today?"

"Would you care to talk to him for yourself?"

"Nah. It's okay. Listen, the reason I called, we've got the official line-up set for Thursday afternoon. It's at four-thirty at headquarters downtown."

"I may have to go to a memorial service. I'm not sure what time it'll be."

"Oh. Sorry. Someone you know died?" There was a brief pause. "Well, that was a stupid question, I'm sure you don't drop in on memorial services just for the hell of it. Let me know as soon as you know, okay? But it might not matter because it's the *official* line-up. We want to do an unofficial one today. This afternoon, if you have time."

"Unofficial line-up?" I asked. Bill quirked an eyebrow at me in inquiry and I shrugged.

"Yeah. We have a suspect in mind. What we'd like is to have you go to Starbucks with me. We'll sit and drink some coffee. This unofficial suspect will go by the store while we're in there. All you have to do is look out the window and tell me if you see anybody you recognize."

"How are you going to swing it?" I mouthed to Bill 'this afternoon'. He nodded in understanding.

Sloan made a noise. I suspected it was a rude one, but I let it pass. "I can manage it. So I'll pick you up at your house at three. Is that okay?"

I nibbled my toast. "Why are we doing this unofficial thing?"

"Because we want to."

"But I don't—"

"So is three okay?"

I started to snap a reply then realized it would be futile. "I have to be back from this Starbuck thing by four-thirty, though. I have a golf tournament tonight."

There was a long pause. Bill gestured to himself then to me and I nodded emphatically. "I need the moral support," I whispered to him. He grinned and winked.

"Okay, I realize Minnesota has some real die-hard golfers, but how are you going to golf in the middle of March?"

"Indoor golf league. Dinner starts at five, tournament starts at six-thirty. It's out at Burnsville Bowl & Drive, on Portland and 13."

"Indoor golf..." Sloan's voice trailed off. "Okay. I'm not going to try to figure that one out. Can anybody drop by and watch?"

"Sure." I fed Magoo some more bacon, ignoring Bill's reproving look.

"I'll be there. If this Starbucks thing works out the way I think it will, I want you to have protection tonight and tomorrow. I suppose Manion will go with you to give you moral and immoral support."

"Hey! No fair eavesdropping!"

"That's what I figured. I'll pick you up for Starbucks at three. See you then." He hung up.

"He's the grumpiest man I've ever met."

"Like I said. He's just jealous." Bill polished off his breakfast and smiled at me.

"You look like the cat who just ate the canary." I munched my toast, giving Magoo a little *'sorry, he's watching'* look.

"I did. In a manner of speaking." He waggled his eyebrows at me. "Let's get this day started so we can get it finished and I can end up in bed with you again."

"You're taking a lot for granted, buster." I stood to clear off the table. Bill looked so worried I started to laugh. "I think you're safe to do so."

"Don't give me heart failure. I'm an old guy. We don't handle surprises very well."

"Really?" I pushed him aside to stack my dishes in the dishwasher. "Do you mean I should forget about pulling out my little Victoria's Secret number tonight when you come to my house to stay over?"

He turned to stare at me. "Some surprises are

just fine."

I dropped Bill at Del's Garage where his truck was being repaired and where he could rent a car. I gave him a long kiss, made him promise to be at my house by four-thirty then shot away in a cloud of snow, tooting the horn as I headed toward the freeway. I drove to work, humming along with Eric Clapton on my CD player. Man, life was good. Wow. Who would think I' be so lucky as to find such a great guy at my stage of life?

According to Kate, *she* did. "I told you," she declared when I appeared at her cube. "There are nice guys in the world. You just have to be willing to take a chance."

"This from the woman who was predicting a hideous end in a chipper/shredder," Ken pointed out from behind her.

I waved them away. "No hideous ends, just happy endings." Then I remembered. "Except for Billy."

"There was no chance for a happy ending there," Kate said. "I talked to Mark. The memorial is scheduled for Thursday at one o'clock. I told him we'd all be there."

"Good." I looked at my desk, computer, and work piled up. "Somehow this stuff doesn't seem all that important. Between Bill and Billy, I've gotten a different perspective on the world."

"He's a good guy?" Ken asked, his dark eyes reflecting his concern.

"One of the best."

"Good. You deserve *the* best, but I'll settle for one of the best. Is he coming to dinner tonight? You are still golfing, right?"

"Oh yeah. I wouldn't miss it." I looked again at my work. "I'll take a stab at this. Then I can take time off with a clear conscience."

Kate waved an airy hand. "Don't worry about it.

What'll they do, fire you? Besides, if they do, who cares? Retire with your handsome mechanic and have fun."

I grinned. "His words exactly."

Ken tugged on Kate's arm. "Sounds like a smart man. We're looking forward to meeting him." He started to edge away, nudging Kate out of the cube.

At two o'clock I went home, placating the Major and Sergeant with lavish petting and full food bowls. Then I changed my clothes, pulling on jeans and my Bloomington Bombshells sweatshirt for the upcoming golf outing. I examined myself critically in the mirror. Not bad for a woman who only had a couple of hours of sleep last night. Thank God I carried a bit of makeup, otherwise I would have frightened Bill over breakfast.

The Bluetooth headset in my ear buzzed, alerting me to an incoming call. "Oh, damn, I really don't want this," I muttered to Snuggle, who watched from the bathtub. She yawned, her pink tongue matching the pink of my wall tiles. "Crisis Cell hotline," I said into the receiver.

"I'm sorry. I don't know what to do."

Oh, shit. It was Tim again. I *really* didn't want to deal with this. "Is this you, Tim? You know it doesn't do you any good to call me. I can't sympathize with your anger. You should call Hal or go into the office and talk to a counselor."

"I know. But something's happened and I don't know what to do."

He sounded truly miserable. I squelched what little sympathy I felt. "I'm going to transfer you to the office. You need to find someone else to talk to."

"I talked to Bill today."

I bounced against the door as I was leaving the bathroom, shock making my legs wobbly. "You did what?"

"I saw him at the bar this noon. I was..." His

voice crackled.

"What the hell was he doing in a bar at noon?" I asked before I could stop myself.

Tim laughed bitterly. "He was looking for me."

"Oh." I went into the living room and stared out the windows to the park beyond. A new blanket of snow had fallen overnight, giving everything the fresh look only new powder can give. "What did you talk about?" He hesitated so long I prompted, "Tim? Are you still there? What did you and Bill talk about?"

"The past. I think I realized..." Once again there an interruption and I didn't hear what Tim said. "...really sorry he had to lay me off. He said it wasn't his decision."

"Well, duh," I said, speaking before I truly thought about my words. "I'm sorry, but you knew better, didn't you?"

"I suppose. And I suppose I just didn't want to think about it." He stalled again; either that, or his phone once again lost the signal.

"You said you had a problem and you didn't know what to do. Are you trying to think how to apologize to Bill?"

"No, nothing like that."

*Asshole,* I thought. "Then what is it?"

"A police detective contacted me today and said he..." Tim's voice vanished briefly then returned. "...catch Bill."

"What? Catch Bill?"

"That's what has me worried. He showed me a search warrant and it looked official but how did he...? And why did he...think...Bill?"

"Bill what?" I demanded again. "This makes no sense, Tim."

"I know. I thought..." His voice faded away briefly. "...too much of a coincidence. After all...tonight and...I had planned to...with her so..."

154

"I can't hear you. Can you go somewhere and use a different phone?"

"...if I do, maybe I'll be able to...I didn't realize he was following...careful because I think he's the one who...tires."

The phone went quiet in my hand.

"Damn!" I shook the phone for good measure, but no sound issued forth. Once again I couldn't share this cryptic conversation with anyone. "Stupid confidentiality agreements." I checked the cell phone's call records and re-dialed the number, but no one answered. Either Tim had the phone off or he was out of service range. I waited for a prompt to leave a message, but never got one.

I heard a car in the driveway. I checked through the kitchen window and saw Detective Sloan getting out of a dark blue Honda Accord. I opened the front door just as Sloan was raising his hand to knock. "Hello, Detective." I grabbed my jacket from the coat rack. "You're on time."

"Punctuality is a virtue." As before, he was dressed in dark jeans, a dark sweater, and a gray jacket. His salt-and-pepper hair looked uncombed and wild.

"Punctuality?" I dragged on my coat as I walked with him to the car. "A polysyllabic word? I'm impressed."

"Polysyllabic?" He tried the pronunciation. "That's a real word?"

"It certainly is." I jerked open the passenger side door and dropped down on the seat. "I have a rhetorical question for you."

"Rhetorical. Another big word. That's like, a pretend question, right? One of those, 'I have a friend who has a problem and I wonder if you can help her' kind of questions?"

I glanced sharply at him but he appeared innocent, smiling politely and nodding in an encouraging fashion. "Yes, in a way."

"Okay, shoot. I'm good at rhetorical questions."

"What if I receive some information in confidence I think may be pertinent to our investigation?"

He backed the car out and put it into drive before answering. "Our investigation? As in, the murder of Jimmy Vann?"

I nodded.

"What kind of 'in confidence' are we talking about here?"

"Well..." I considered. "Like the kind of confidence I gave you. Professional. Let's say someone told you something but you're bound by...whatever, your oath of office or professional ethics or...whatever, and you're not supposed to tell anybody."

"Hmm. That's tricky. It's 'seal of confessional' stuff, unless you're slapped with a court order, in which case you have to decide whether to go to jail or not. Me, personally—I'd cough up the information rather than go to jail. But I'm wimpy that way." He glanced at me as we merged onto Main Street. "What's at stake? If you don't tell what you know, what might happen? Is somebody in danger?"

"I'm not sure. That's what has me so worried." I tapped an impatient finger on the door handle, trying to replay my conversation with Tim in my mind. "The information I got was cryptic at best, and I may be misinterpreting it."

"Hmm. Trickier and trickier. I have to say, unless you're sure someone might be injured or be in danger, then I'm not sure you'd have a legal leg to stand on."

"I'm not talking legality. I'm talking...well, ethics." I considered. "And I suppose there might be a legal issue, too. Oh. That reminds me." I checked the Crisis Cell, setting it so it would answer automatically and transfer to my headset. That way I could golf without having to worry about being thumped.

He grinned. "You're talking to the wrong person about ethics. I either slept through the class in college or was out playing football. Sorry, Mary Madison. I'm not sure I can help you with your problem. This might be one of those things where you have to go with your gut...again."

He was probably right but I hated to admit it. I tried another tack. "You didn't by any chance contact a..." I struggled to find an appropriate word, "...ex-co-worker of Bill's and ask him to assist us, did you?"

We rolled to a stop at a traffic light and he shot me a disbelieving look. "Contact who? Ask him to do what?"

"I didn't think so," I said glumly. Tim had said something about 'tonight'. Well, I had that covered. Bill would be with me at the tournament and then we'd spend the evening together. Therefore I didn't have to worry about tonight. As long as I stayed on my toes and kept an eye on things, we'd be fine. I repeated the words to myself a couple of more times, hoping conviction would sink in.

It didn't work. I gave up on reassurance and decided to comfort myself with a memory of Bill. That tactic worked and my troubles dissolved.

"I'll figure it out," I said. "Hey, the light's green. Let's go get some coffee and catch bad guys, Detective Sloan."

Chapter 13

"What aren't you telling me, Mary Madison?" Sloan let up on the brake and we moved forward. "Did someone call you again? Did somebody say something about Manion?"

"It's nothing. Really. Like I said, I don't have all the information so I'm just not going to worry about it. I shouldn't have mentioned anything."

"Hmm." He glanced a couple of times at me but didn't press it. "So I take it Manion isn't the worse for wear because of his accident?"

I smiled out my window. "You could say so."

"Did you have a good time last night? I mean, I don't want to be nosy, but he and I talked about a...problem and I was sort of..."

I decided to help dig Sloan out of the social hole he'd dug for himself. I flashed him a beaming smile. "Whoever implied Bill had problems was vastly mistaken. Spurious and scurrilous, completely."

Sloan's jaw dropped. "Spurious?"

I nodded. "And scurrilous."

He shot me a narrow-eyed stare. "Write that down. I want to look those words up." He took a left turn onto busy Highway 7, which would lead us out of town. "So it was a total lie?"

I smiled at the snowy day. "Completely unfounded."

"Maybe it's just the company he keeps."

"Maybe. I never thought of myself as femme fatale material but maybe I am."

"Folks get to a certain age and perceptions start to change. I used to love short redheads with big boobs." He shrugged. "Now I like some gray in the hair and a nice, trim figure. But I still have a weakness for redheads, I have to admit." He glanced at me and I know he was eyeing my red/gray hair-do.

I smiled wryly. "There's a woman out there for you, Detective. It's just a matter of being open to the possibilities. That's what happened with me." I stared at the Starbucks as we drove past it. "You missed our coffee shop."

"We're going to a different one," Sloan said. "So is this thing with Manion serious? You know, are you going to settle down?"

I shrugged. "Who knows? We barely know each other. We'll see what works out."

"There aren't any guarantees on this stuff, Mary Madison." Sloan steered onto the freeway and merged with traffic. "Trust your instincts."

I considered his words. Sloan had been right so far, but marriage? I wasn't ready for that step yet. I wasn't ready to even think about it yet. I shook the speculation aside. I had other things to worry about today. "So how does this work? Did you ask various people to come by and parade in front of the coffee shop?"

"Please. You're smarter than that. We're smarter than that." He took the 66th Street exit.

"The royal 'we'?" I grinned at him.

"You might say so. Captain Salisbury set this up. In the next hour or so, five detectives are due to walk by the front window of the coffee shop, all on legitimate police business."

"Clever." I glanced at him as we drove down the four-lane street. "And you trust him? You trust this Captain Salisbury?"

Sloan's surprised look told me he didn't think I could put the facts together. "What's that mean?"

"Just if he's targeted five people, then he must have a suspect in mind. If he has a suspect in mind, then I wonder why the hell he isn't looking at them a bit closer. What's he waiting for?"

Sloan turned into a small strip mall. "Sal may have somebody in mind, but he's not sharing and I'm not going to pry. He can handle it his way, as long as my witness isn't put into any danger."

"Thanks," I said as we pulled into a parking space. "Nice to know you're looking out for my interests."

"Believe me, I am."

We went into the shop and Sloan directed me to a table they'd picked out. He got us coffee then settled down across from me, his back to the window. "Okay, just keep your eye on the window over my right shoulder and tell me if you see somebody you know." He nudged one cup of coffee toward me.

"This is very clever. With the darkened windows, he won't be able to see me. I presume we're trying to narrow down the field?" I sipped my coffee, my eyes meeting his.

"Watch the window."

I jerked my gaze to the glass. "Sorry."

"We've got a couple of suspects in mind. This is a way for us to make sure we watch the right people. We don't want to lose this guy."

I nodded and sipped the coffee, my eyes glued to the window. "So he's been under suspicion for a while?"

"Sort of."

"Hmm." I eyed the people hurrying by the window. "That one looks like him but..." I sipped my coffee. Sloan touched the fork on the table. "Is that a clue?" I asked. "Are there other people here who are watching?"

"Yep. I can't exactly run out and tail the guy. We're keeping an eye on him, remember?"

"Oh, of course." I longed to look behind me at the other coffee shop patrons, but didn't dare. Sloan was staring at me intently. I eyed the man in the parking lot. "No, it's not him but it's very like him. The round-faced man was taller and broader."

I sipped my coffee and waited. "So did you find out who left those fingerprints on my car? Did you check the fingerprints against any of these people I'm looking at today?" I deliberately kept my gaze on the window, but I saw Sloan's blue eyes zeroing in on me from my peripheral vision.

"All we got was a partial," he said. "Not enough for a positive identification."

"Hmm." I sipped my coffee. "I've been thinking about the tires."

"Really?"

"Yeah. It doesn't quite make sense. I mean, if the Bad Guy—let's call him BG for short—if BG knows who I am, why didn't he just come to my house and get me?" I glanced quickly at Sloan, who was regarding me with his 'where is she going with this now?' look. "I think I know what happened."

"Do you? Pray tell. Elaborate."

"Two polysyllabic words in an hour. My, my. It must be the company you keep."

He snorted. "It's rubbing off on me, I guess."

I settled back in my chair and stretched out my snow clogs toward the fireplace where the faux flames flickered. "Let's say BG is worried I might identify him. Maybe he hung around the garage or

161

the hospital last Wednesday, waiting to see if I came out." I sipped some more coffee, sorting through facts and ideas in my brain. I was considering all of this, off and on, for almost a week and I *think* I had it figured out. "So let's say he hangs around the garage and he sees me. He might have even seen me with Bill. Maybe he saw me get into my car and got the license number."

"There's a lot of 'maybe' there. But if he got your license number then, why didn't he—"

I held up a cautionary finger. "Just wait. Maybe that's what he did."

"What?"

"He waited. He waited to see if I reported him. Then we saw him, or rather *I* saw him, on Friday night at the police place. It probably convinced him I was a viable witness, I was somebody to worry about. But..."

"But? Keep going. You're spinning a nice story here."

I shot Sloan a quick look then focused once again on the window. "Nobody arrested him. So that had BG wondering—what part did I have in all this? Was anybody taking me seriously? I didn't have police protection. I didn't have a guard. Why not? What's the deal? So he decided to test his theory. He decided to see if I was being kept hidden."

Sloan smiled slowly. "So he slashed your tires."

"Yep. What would normally happen if somebody vandalized a car? Don't answer, it's a rhetorical question."

"Yeah. I recognize it."

I ignored Sloan's sarcastic reply and kept going. I was on a roll and wanted to test my theory on somebody who understood police procedure and the way a criminal would think. "If vandalism occurred, that person would report it to the local police. They'd call the Chaska police, where the vandalism occurred. Somebody said that to me. They asked why I called you in particular. Why didn't I just call the local cops?"

"Who suggested it?"

I stared out the window. "That might be him." I watched a stocky man in a blue jacket walk across my field of vision, talking to another man. Something was not quite right about him, though. His hair was the wrong color and not the right texture. "Nope," I said. "Wrong hair. BG didn't have lay-down hair, he had spiky hair."

"Take your time. No rush."

"Nope. It's not him. So where was I? Oh, yeah. The tires. When you didn't file a report, it confirmed it for BG I was important. Because you handled it yourself and because you tried to keep it a secret." I glanced at Sloan, whose face appeared frozen with disbelief. "Now BG knows I'm a real witness." I sipped my coffee, remembering the panic I felt on Sunday night. "He tried to check my house but I saw the lights and you sent a squad car over there."

From the corner of my eye, I saw Sloan nod. I took it for tacit assent and forged ahead. "I was with Bill on Saturday. Saturday night the tires were slashed and you didn't file a police report. I haven't been alone since then. You and I got home late on Sunday after talking to Bill, you had scared him away on Sunday night, I was at work on Monday, and last night I was with Bill." I dared a quick glance at Sloan, who was staring thoughtfully at his coffee cup. "BG has to be getting desperate. He's got to be worried. You said something about an *official* police lineup?"

"Hunh?"

"How do they do these lineups? Do they ask police officers to participate? Do you have a regular group of people you pull in and ask them to fill in?"

Sloan pulled out a small memo book from his

jacket pocket and flipped it open. "We usually ask for a few volunteers who resemble the description. You know, 'anybody who's between five-foot-ten and six-foot with black hair and who owns a gray jacket, report to—you get the idea." He pulled a pen out of a holder on the memo book and started writing. "But sometimes we ask specific people to come in, too. That way we're sure to get the right pool."

"So a memo has gone out and BG now knows you're looking for somebody who might look like him." I eyed two men coming toward me from across the parking lot. I shook my head. I could tell by the walk, neither man was BG. "Maybe he was even specially invited to this little party. He knows you're closing in. That's the royal 'you', by the way."

A quick grin told me Sloan heard. I picked up my coffee stirrer and idly tapped it on the table. "So it means tonight might be the night." My hand paused as I stared at another man coming toward us. "That might be... Nope. Sorry."

"You're doing fine. You'll be good on the witness stand." Sloan leaned back and put his notepad away.

"Witness stand? Like in court? Wow. I guess I didn't think that far ahead." I hazarded a glance at him. "Interesting."

"Trust me. It's also boring."

"I think that's him," I said, spotting a man in a dark gray coat who paused outside the window, talking to a smaller Asian man. "He's got one of those scruffy beards now and his hair is shorter. I think he had longer hair." He and the other man talked for a moment then the Caucasian man walked away. "It's him," I said. "He had a bouncy walk and the shoulders are right. Just the beard is different."

Sloan lifted the fork and started tapping it against the table. A woman got up next to us and left the shop. "I thought women liked those scruffy beards," he commented, glancing at the man who'd been sitting with the woman and nodding.

"Only in the morning." I remembered Bill's scratchy face and how he'd sandpapered my breasts. I leaned over the table. "Aren't you going to chase that man? I'm sure it's him."

"It's being handled," Sloan said. "We sit here for a while then I'll take you home and wait with you until your hot date comes to pick you up. Then we'll all go golfing together."

I considered his comment, head tilted to one side. "Do you think I'm in danger?"

"I wouldn't say danger, exactly."

"What would you say?"

"We're just being cautious. We're cops. We're like that."

I sipped my coffee. "Do I really have to testify at a trial?"

Sloan shrugged. "Depends on what our guy does. All you can do is put him in the garage at the time of the murder. That's not enough for a conviction."

I thought it over. "So you're hoping to scare him out into the open? You're hoping he'll make a mistake?" Sloan nodded. "Isn't it a bit risky?"

"He's good. He's covered it up. We don't have much else to go on."

"He sounds smart."

Sloan smiled. "We're smarter." He was watching the man at the table next to us. Some signal must have been passed because he stood. "Time to go now. So tell me about this golf stuff tonight. How does it work?"

We chatted about the tournament all the way back to my house where Bill was waiting for us. He came to meet the car as we pulled into the drive, leaning over to talk to Sloan.

"Something happened today you need to know about."

"Let's talk inside," I suggested, getting out of Sloan's car. I led the way to the house and we all went inside, standing in the entryway next to the kitchen.

"I went down to Benteen's today," Bill said, reaching out an arm and tugging me close to him. "I wanted to see who might be spreading rumors about me."

I looked up at him in surprise. "Was it that CiCi girl?"

He nodded. "And Tim McIntyre." His hand tightened on my shoulder. "He said you and he have chatted."

I touched the Crisis Cell at my waistband. "It's confidential. I told you." I was getting dizzy trying to remember who said what and what I could say to who.

"I know. I'm not blaming you."

"So what did this McIntyre guy say?" Sloan prompted, hands jammed deeply into his jacket pockets.

"He blames me for his troubles." Bill frowned. "For everything that happened to him."

"And...?" Sloan prompted.

"When I got done talking to him, I checked out back, behind the bar. His brown pickup truck was in the parking lot."

I saw the interested expression in Sloan's blue eyes. "Really? The vehicle that hit you had a brown fender," he said. "I checked the police report."

"Yeah, how about it? Tim's truck also has a smashed fender on the front driver's side. Just like the truck that hit me."

"Mystery solved," Sloan said, pulling out his cell phone. "I'm going to follow up on it. I'll meet you guys at the bowling alley or driving range or whatever it's called."

"One mystery solved," I corrected. "There're still

the slashed tires." I looked at Bill, who nodded.

"You're right. I don't think Tim did that."

I met Sloan's eyes and I saw my thoughts reflected in his baby blues. *Let's not get Bill worried about that.* Sloan nodded. "Let's take our mysteries one at a time."

## Chapter 14

"He's not bad looking," Marge said an hour later as she looked at Bill, chatting with Steven by the dessert bar. "The bruise gives him a rugged look. And his nose is cute."

We were sitting in the restaurant attached to the bowling alley where my tournament was being held. "He said he broke it when he was young and it never got set right." I watched Bill as he leaned over to drop a dollop of whipped cream on his hot fudge sundae.

"He could be a serial killer and you wouldn't know," Barb insisted. "You just don't know about people anymore."

"He doesn't look like a serial killer," Peggy pointed out.

"How many serial killers do you know?" Mary Jane asked.

"Hell, Bruce Springsteen looks like a serial killer," Marge said. "Especially when he's got his hair all slicked back. Like the *Tunnel of Love* album."

"That's what I told Kate," I said around a mouthful of ice cream.

"You told me what?" Kate demanded from the other side of the big table.

"About serial killers and how Bruce looks like one."

"You did. And you were right."

Barb snorted. "You can't tell and that's that. All you can do is go by feelings. Always trust your feelings." Six pairs of eyes swung to pin me to my chair. "What do they tell you?"

"They tell me he's a sweet guy and I'm lucky to have him."

"Hmm." Barb continued to regard Bill with cool suspicion. "What did he do at Deere?"

"He was a foreman in the machine shop."

There was dead silence around the table. "That's nice," Peggy said.

"A man who knows tools," Marge said with satisfaction. "Useful. I don't know about you, but the older I get, the sexier a tool belt looks."

I looked at Marge and Peggy gratefully, knowing exactly what everyone was thinking. *What do you and he have in common?' You have two Ph.D.s, what the hell are you doing hanging out with some mechanic?'*

"He's nice. And he's sweet and we do fun things."

"What do you mean, *'you do fun things'?"* Mary Jane demanded. "I thought this was your first date?"

"Not exactly." I moved my chair slightly so Bill could slip into the seat next to me.

We all turned and smiled in unison with varying degrees of sincerity. Ken ignored us and concentrated on his food. Bill sat down next to me and his dark eyes were laughing as he asked, "Did I pass inspection?"

Marge and Peggy grinned. Barb regarded him coolly and said, "We're not sure, frankly. After all, Threemie deserves only the best."

Bill nodded agreement. "I understand. She sets a high standard for me to live up to." He looked sideways at me but I was glaring at my friends. His leg pressed against mine under the table and my hand, already hidden under the tablecloth, rested on his thigh. "I think Threemie and I have a lot to teach each other. I know I have a lot to learn from her, at least. By the way, how many degrees *do* you have?" He turned his dark blue eyes on me.

I just shrugged and sipped my wine.

"As long as you know she's special," Barb stated, obviously making up her mind he was acceptable.

Mary Jane gave him a narrow-eyed look. "If you hurt her, you'll be in deep shit."

He nodded and took a bite of sundae, choking as my hand moved up his leg under the tablecloth. "Be nice," he warned.

I gave his thigh a long, evaluating squeeze. "Always." I looked around at the circle of Pubs people who came out to cheer me at the tournament and raised my coffee mug. "Here's to new friends and fun times."

"Hear, hear!" several people shouted drunkenly.

Steven leaned over and whispered, "He said he'd check my car."

I looked toward heaven, asking for patience. As I did, I saw a woman standing on the other side of the restaurant, eyeing us. The way she was giving me the once-over made the hair on the back of my neck stand up. "I guess we're making too much noise."

Bill followed my stare and this time he did choke on his food. "Holy shit."

"You know her?"

"Yeah. I did." He watched as the woman sauntered across the restaurant. As she neared our table, I saw she was wearing the same clothing as the waitresses. She came up on Bill's left side, insinuating herself between him and me.

"Hey, Bill," she said in a dark, throaty voice.

Marge, Kate, Barb, Peggy, Mary Jane, and I all assessed her with one scathing glance and exchanged loaded looks: *slut*. Ken and Steven, who had been around all of us long enough to be attuned to our moods, looked interested at the potential for a female explosion.

"Hey, Crystal," Bill said. "I didn't know you worked here."

I almost dropped my coffee. This was the mysterious Crystal, she who was into BDSM. I suddenly wondered if she enjoyed being the dominated or the dominator. After spending the night with Bill, I couldn't really imagine him in either role but I know which one I'd prefer. I shivered at the thought.

The woman nodded, shifting her weight onto one hip. "I've worked here for a year now." She glanced down at me then locked her gaze back on Bill. The dismissal was obvious. I started to smolder. "I haven't seen you around town much lately. I heard you retired."

Bill pushed back from the table, putting distance between himself and the tall blonde bitch who was nearly leaning on him. As he did, he saw my glare. "Threemie, this is Crystal. I think I mentioned her to you once." His dark navy eyes met mine and flashed with laughter. "When we were talking about personal preferences." He quirked an eyebrow. "Crystal, this is a good friend of mine. Mary Madison."

Crystal's blue eyes narrowed with suspicion. She glanced at me. "Hey."

I looked up at her, then to Bill. "Hey."

"You go, girl," Barb whispered next to me.

"I'd better get back to work," Crystal said, edging away from Bill. She gave him a long, simmering smile. "Call me sometime. Maybe we can have a drink for old times." Her raking glance over Bill's body left no doubt as to what else they might have for old times.

"I'm usually busy." He smiled at me. "In fact, isn't it time we went next door and got ready for your tournament?"

Crystal glanced over her shoulder at me, gave me one evaluating look, then her blue-shadowed eyes landed back on Bill. "Really? Well, if you get a chance, give me a call." She sauntered away, hips swaying in the tight black skirt.

"Hussy," I whispered.

Bill laughed. "We didn't have that great a time when we were together. She's not interested in me calling her. She's just trying to stir things up."

I shot him an intent, narrow-eyed stare. "It's not her I'm wondering about."

He leaned over and put a hand on my neck, drawing me to him. "I asked you to marry me this morning. Surely that counts for something? I'm not making any phone calls unless it's to you, sugar." He pulled me to him and we kissed.

After a shocked silence, several voices shouted, "You're getting married?"

I stared into his eyes. "I believe you. Sorry. It's just hard after what happened with Jack."

He nodded then we both looked at the stunned people sitting around the table. "We're thinking about getting engaged," Bill explained. He turned back to his sundae, smiling at the bombshell he'd just dropped.

"Considering it," I agreed.

Steven beamed at me. "Excellent. A mechanic for life."

"And what will you do to earn such a reward?" I demanded.

"Plan your wedding, of course." Steven leaned toward Bill. "She has very little style sense, you

172

know. If you want a nice event, you'd better let us do it."

"You're jumping the gun. We're not to the planning stage."

"What stage are we at?" Bill asked, a twinkle in his eye.

"The evaluation stage."

"Ooh, nice stage," Marge said. "You should stay there for a while, try out the product, make sure it's suitable."

"I'm not even going to discuss..." I got to my feet. "Time to go play golf."

"You're changing the subject again," Bill noted as we gathered coats.

"Not at all. I just need to gear up for my competition. I'm a bit nervous about this tonight," I said as we pulled on our coats to go next door to the bowling alley/golf facility. "It's Oakmont. I'm no good on Oakmont. It's so damn hilly. And there's the Church Pew Bunker, between 3 and 4. I hate that bunker."

"They have famous courses?" he asked as we emerged into the cold March night.

"Yeah, we're playing the Cedar Falls Fillies tonight and they chose it." I frowned at the light snow starting to fall. "I'm getting tired of snow."

Bill put an arm around me. "Not too long to go. It's March. Pretty soon we'll take my Mustang out for a spin." We went to Bill's truck and he retrieved my clubs, glancing around the lot. I followed his glance. There were no brown trucks, round-faced men, or anything unusual. I led the way into the building to my team, gathered around a large table in the middle of the golf area with pitchers of beer next to the pizza on the table.

"Threemie!!" A shout went up as I appeared, shaking snow out of my hair. Then all eyes turned to Bill, who smiled.

"You brought a caddy," my playing partner, Beth, commented as Bill put my clubs against a low dividing wall where other clubs were set. Then she looked at the Pubs people crowding in after me. "And a cheering section. What is this, Threemie's Army?"

"This is Bill," I said. "He's a friend of mine. And those are guys from work."

Bill turned to face my team as I introduced them, finishing with, "Everybody, this is Bill." I waved to the other Pubs people, who were all pulling up chairs, shedding coats, and calling out for beer. "And there's Marge and Steven and Ken and... Ah, hell, just introduce yourselves."

"Do you drink beer, Bill?" Beth's husband asked, holding up an empty glass.

"Sure do," Bill said, pulling out a chair and sitting down.

"You'll fit right in."

I huddled with Beth, my Best Ball partner for the night and Delores and Sally, our team captains. They informed me our venue had changed. "We're playing Pebble Beach instead of Oakmont," I said in disgust when I finally broke away to talk to Bill.

"Nice course." He peered over my shoulder at the driving range, an open space with six rear-projection screens.

"See, that's how it works." I nodded toward a man who was teeing off. He took a full swing with a driver and his golf ball slammed into the soft screen. As it did, the image on the screen changed to the new location on the fairway. "In Minnesota, golf is an option for six months out of the year unless you're a die-hard golfer." I grinned. "And I'm not. I use the indoor matches to keep my swing loosened up during the dead of winter."

He turned his attention back to me. "So you're on Pebble Beach tonight?"

I nodded. "I always screw up on number eight.

I'm glad you came with me. It's nice to have a special cheering section."

He kissed the tip of my nose. "I'll always cheer you on, Threemie."

My Bombshell teammates exchanged looks with the Pubs people, all nudging each other. I would have plenty of questions to answer tomorrow. Then I looked at Bill and decided he was worth the interrogation.

I looked up as Marcus Sloan pulled a chair over and sat down.

"Hey, when's the game start?" he asked.

"Match," Bill corrected. He gestured to the large group of people all gathered around the table, arguing, talking, or gesturing. "Threemie's Army."

"How did the thing go this afternoon?" I asked. "Is it wrapped up?"

Sloan took a slice of pizza and shrugged. Bill leaned back in his chair and stretched out his legs. "Does that mean everything's okay?"

"We're working on it," Sloan said around a bit of food. He nodded toward me. "Let's just not leave our girl alone tonight."

"Not on your life." Bill winked at me.

"Well, let's get started, team," Delores said as she stood up. "Let's whup some butt."

"You're on." I bounded to my feet and led the way to the chairs behind the low dividing wall separating the driving area from the café side. Bill settled into a chair with Pubs people around him, the beer in front of them on top of the short wall. Sloan stood to one side, munching pizza and glancing from me to the bowling alley side of the facility.

The match got underway and I focused on staying competitive. By the end of five holes, Beth and I were ahead. I came over to get a refill on my beer. "Looks like we've got company," I said, peering over Bill's shoulder.

He followed my look. Crystal was leaning against the bar, sipping a glass of wine. Several men were eyeing her and I could see why. She'd changed into skin-tight blue jeans, a short red sweater, and her blonde hair was piled in a tumbled mass on top of her head, making her look like she'd just rolled out of bed.

I looked down at my faded denims and loose sweatshirt. I knew how my hair looked—flyaway, not sexy-tumbled.

Bill turned back to me. "She doesn't know how to golf."

I looked past him to Crystal, who was watching us with a smug smile. "Looks like she knows how to do some other things," I snapped.

Bill stared into my eyes. "She sure as hell doesn't make me sit up and take notice the way you do," he said in a low, husky voice.

I smiled. "I guess this old redhead can show that brown-root blonde a thing or two?"

Bill laughed out loud. "You bet, honey." He patted me on the ass as I went back to the match. I glanced over my shoulder and saw Crystal's disgusted look. I gave a little wiggle as I lined up my next shot.

When I came back for a sip of beer a few minutes later, I looked at the bar and saw Crystal talking to a man—someone I recognized. "Holy buckets," I said to Bill. "Look."

He and Sloan both turned in their chairs. "Tim," Bill said softly. "What's he doing here?"

"Coincidence?" I asked.

"I don't believe in coincidence," Sloan muttered, getting up.

"Don't," I said. "The poor man's got enough problems."

"Hey, he hurt your boyfriend here. Not to

mention slander." Sloan looked from me to Bill. "It's your call."

"Let me talk to him," I said. "We'll take a break in a few minutes, after the front nine. Maybe he'll talk to me." I touched Bill's arm. "Please. If he did hurt you, he should pay, but I'd like to—" What? I don't know what I wanted, but I didn't want that poor man to be hurt any more than he had been. I also wanted to find out what he knew. If I could get Tim to reveal more information in the company of Sloan or Bill, then I was off the confidentiality hook.

Bill must have read my thoughts. "He needs counseling or something." He smiled briefly and I know he was just humoring me. "And you're a counselor so I guess I can't say no."

"Thanks. Just give me a minute or two."

"I still say..."

I tuned out Sloan's objection as I walked back to the match. I was facing the dreaded eighth hole and I needed all my wits about me in order to drive my tee shot into the correct spot to set Beth up for a chance at the green.

The damn ocean beckoned to me from the left as I took aim. I glanced at Bill and smiled. I took a deep breath and swung.

We survived eight with a bogey five and finished nine at two under par, two shots ahead of our competitors. I was pleased with our play, given that I kept glancing over my shoulder to verify Tim was still there and Sloan hadn't taken him out in handcuffs.

I set down my putter and joined Bill. Sloan was nowhere in sight. "Where's our bodyguard?" I asked, checking the bar area. Tim was still there and he was talking to Crystal.

"He got a call. Somebody got shot a few blocks away and he had to go."

"Wow. I wonder what happened. This is a pretty

safe part of town." I sipped my beer, relief washing over me. If Sloan could vanish, then obviously there wasn't anything to worry about. I said as much to Bill.

"Maybe. But I still don't want you out of my sight."

I gestured toward Tim, who was watching us through the smoky haze surrounding the pool tables. "I'm just going over there."

"Threemie."

I stopped and looked at Bill.

"If he did run into my truck, Tim has to pay for what he did. I could have been hurt a lot worse than I was."

I nodded, remembering the bruises on Bill's body. "I know that." I left before I blurted out anything I was told in confidence. I suspect Tim was already regretting his actions, and I was hoping it might mitigate any punishment he'd receive.

Crystal meandered away as I approached them. Tim turned bleary eyes on me. He looked terrible—pale and drawn, as though he hadn't slept in days. His hand trembled as he lifted the beer mug.

"We need to talk, Tim," I said without preamble.

He lowered the mug and almost fumbled it. I caught it in time to prevent him from sloshing it all over the bar. "I'm in trouble," he said in a slurred voice. "Big trouble."

"Well, I think we can talk to Bill. He'll be reasonable. I think if you agree to go to counseling and maybe make restitution, he'll—"

"Not that," Tim said in a low, anxious voice. He looked beyond me, his watering eyes searching frantically around the bar. "A cop is after me."

"Detective Sloan? I don't think so. Besides, he had to leave, he's—"

"Not that cop. The other one. He told me if I didn't help him, he'd arrest me."

"What?" I replayed our earlier fragmented conversation in my mind. "You said something about a search warrant? Is someone searching your house?"

"Not my house. Bill's. Tonight." He looked past me, his gaze furtive. "Crystal is really pissed off at you and Bill. She's going to get even."

My head was spinning. "Back up. Someone is going to search Bill's house. Why?"

"The detective said tax evasion. All I had to do was distract Bill a bit and they'd have time to execute the warrant."

"That makes no sense. He has to be there when they do it. Otherwise it's breaking and entering." I wasn't certain of this, but it seemed logical. Of course, it was a legal point. It didn't have to be logical. "Tax evasion? That's ridiculous. Did you see this detective's identification? When did he see you?" Then a more pertinent question struck me. "Why did he see you? Why ask you to help?"

Tim nodded. "I know. I thought it was weird. I think the detective could tell I wasn't buying it. That's when he talked to Crystal. She's going to do it." His voice was so low I could barely hear him above the buzz of conversation in the bar.

"Do what? Talked to her when?"

Tim took a deep breath. "I don't know. All I know is she's going to do something."

I glanced back at my golfing contingent, but they were still on a break, milling around the chairs where the beer sat. I tried to spot Bill but didn't see him.

A terrible thought hit me and I whirled, looking around the bar. I didn't see Crystal, either.

That's when somebody screamed.

## Chapter 15

At first I thought the sound was part of a video game or was coming from the TV, but the startled looks on the faces of patrons near the exit told me it was coming from outside. The door suddenly burst open and Crystal staggered inside, her pants unzipped and her sweater pushed up over her breasts, which spilled out of her bra.

I was too far away to hear what she said but she gestured frantically to the door. A barmaid pushed through the gathering crowd and put an arm around the sobbing woman, tugging her sweater down so her boobs were covered. I turned to Tim but he had slipped off his barstool and was making his way to the fringe of the crowd.

I struggled to see over the sea of heads but finally gave up. I turned to go back to my golfing buddies when I saw Bill being dragged in from outside, one of the bartenders locking Bill's arms behind him and pushing him into the bar.

"Oh, shit." It suddenly made sense. That damn bitch Crystal.

I elbowed my way through the crowd, earning a few startled, 'Hey, watch it!' and 'Who do you think you are?' exclamations. I burst through a circle of men surrounding Bill and the bartender, almost catapulting into them.

"...can handle it," the bartender was saying. "Save your story for them."

"Bill, what happened?"

"I didn't do a damn thing, Threemie. Believe me." He looked desperate, frightened, and angry all at once.

I touched his arm in sympathy and looked at the bartender. "He's with me. He didn't do anything."

"That's not what she said." The big man looked at Crystal, crying onto the shoulder of a huge burly man who was glaring at Bill with hatred in his eyes. "We'll let the cops sort this out."

"There's a cop with me," I said, looking around for Sloan. Then I remembered. Damn. "He'll be back soon. Talk to him about it."

"I called it in," the other bartender said. "The local police will be here in a few minutes."

"I didn't do anything," Bill said, struggling to get away from his captor. He winced and I glared at the man holding him.

"He was hurt in an accident yesterday, let him go."

"Threemie, what is it, what's happening?"

I saw Steven and Marge pushing through the crowd toward us. The bartender loosened his hold on Bill's arm slightly, allowing Bill to stand straighter. "I didn't do anything, Threemie," he said desperately. "You have to believe me."

I glanced at Crystal. Her face was pressed against her rescuer's chest, turned slightly toward us. I'm sure only I saw the malicious gleam in her mascara-smeared eyes.

"I'm sure you didn't," I said loudly, praying she would hear. "Everybody knows about her. Good God, her file at the clinic is two inches thick. The doctors have her on a watch list, for cryin' out loud."

A shocked gasp and sudden silence told me my words had penetrated at least some of the conversation around us. Crystal's head snapped up so fast I thought I heard her neck vertebrae pop. "What did you say?" she demanded, all trace of tears and fright vanishing.

"You heard me," I said in a low voice, advancing on her.

"Uh, Threemie." Steven put a restraining hand on my arm.

"Let go of me." I pulled against his grasp.

"She's six inches taller than you and weighs a whole lot more. Be careful."

"Who are you calling fat, you little faggot?" Crystal pulled away from the big guy who'd been holding her and glared at us.

"Who are you calling a faggot?" somebody in the crowd shouted.

"Yeah," Steven said, releasing me and glaring at her. "Who are you calling a faggot?"

"I saw the way you acted at dinner," Crystal spat. "And look at you."

Several people evaluated Steven with his long dark hair, wire-rimmed glasses, and baggy clothes.

"And?" I asked. "I don't see the tattoo that says 'Gay'." Somebody behind me laughed.

"He's wearing an earring." Crystal said it as though it mattered.

"So?" The bartender released Bill and leaned past him to look at Crystal. I saw the small gold earring encircling his right earlobe.

"It's in his right ear. You know what that means." Crystal crossed her arms under her breasts, giving them a lift because her bra was out of service. It only emphasized how badly they were sagging.

A man behind Steven stepped forward. He was easily six-and-a-half feet tall, broad as a barn, with hands the size of small hams. He also wore an earring in his right ear. "So?" he asked, his voice a low growl. "Are you saying I'm gay because I wear an earring?"

All hell broke loose.

Somebody bumped me from behind and I went flying, pushed into a press of people and almost going down. I grabbed for anything to keep me upright and discovered I'd grabbed somebody's thigh. "Sorry," I shouted over the din, letting go and staggering to find my balance. I saw Bill, released from his captor and pushing people aside as he looked through the crowd, searching for me.

I was bumped again and spun, then I saw a clear spot and made a break for it. I dodged two men who were pushing each other, then slammed into the bar. Pain shot up my arm but I kept going. The door to the exit was just a few steps away, and I considered using it but people were spilling out of the doorway and I was afraid of being sucked along in their wake and run over. I aimed for the drop-gate leading into the bar. If I could get under its confines, I wouldn't be trampled. I was almost there when someone grabbed my arm in a vise-like grip. "Hey!" I shouted, struggling to get away. "Let go of me."

He pulled me, hard, until I was upright. That's when I saw who had me.

It was the round-faced man.

"Let's go." He pulled me toward the door.

"No way!" I dug in my heels but he over-balanced me, giving me such a jerk I almost landed face-first on the dirty snow outside the doorway. Two men were fighting in the parking lot and others were running away, heading for cars. Sirens wailed in the distance.

"Help!" I screamed. "Help, I don't want to go with—"

The world went black.

\*\*\*\*

"Are you okay?"

A voice was whispering in my head.

"Miss Madison, are you okay?"

I opened my eyes. Flickering light shone overhead. I was lying down on something springy and cloth-covered. I could feel it under my cheek. I tried to reach in front of me, but my hands were constrained somehow.

Damn. I was tied. And I was in a car. I could see the front seat ahead of me.

"Miss Madison?"

The Crisis Cell headset was still in my right ear. I shifted position slightly so the mike would be able to pick up my voice. "Where am I?" I asked groggily. "What did you do?"

"I don't know what happened," the voice in my ear said. "I'm following you."

"I drugged you. You're going to be taking a little trip." The voice drifted back to me from the front seat.

"A trip? Where? What do you mean you drugged me?"

"I heard that," the voice in my ear whispered. "Who is it?"

"Who are you?" I tried to sit up but it was hard without the use of my hands. I finally managed to get myself propped against the door so I could peer into the front seat. Pain lanced through my head and I winced.

"It's Tim," the voice in my ear said. "I'm following you."

"How did you—?" I stopped myself in time.

My captor didn't notice my gaff. "I drugged you." The man glanced over his right shoulder then faced front again. "Chan was right. One whiff of that stuff worked as good as a shot."

"Where are you taking me?" I almost asked,

*What are you going to do?*, but I was too much of a coward to hear the answer.

Maybe he could read my mind. "I'm going to stash you with some friends of mine, going back across the Canadian border tonight. They'll keep you under wraps long enough for me to get to Thailand."

"Thailand?" I asked in disbelief.

"Oh, my God, he's taking you to Thailand?" Tim asked in my ear. "That's impossible, isn't it? I mean, wouldn't he need a passport or..."

I tuned out Tim and focused on my captor, who was still talking. "I've got a nice little hideaway all set up. No one will find me. Hell, nobody will even look hard. Nobody wants a scandal for the department. Sal will let it die down."

I think he was talking just to convince himself, but I didn't believe him. I have to admit, though, I wasn't really thinking straight. The pain in my head was almost overwhelming and I was seeing double whenever I looked out the front windshield. "Marcus Sloan will look for me, and so will Bill. It won't die down. And if you hurt me, it'll only go harder for you." I hoped I sounded tougher than I felt.

"I'm not going to hurt you."

"You're on the highway going south," Tim whispered. "I'm two cars behind you. I saw you guys leaving the bar." He coughed, the sound echoing terribly in the headset.

"I wish I could talk to Sloan," I muttered. "If I could talk to Sloan, you'd be in deep shit."

"It won't happen. He's busy. My partner, Martin Tsang, got hurt tonight. I made sure it happened where Sloan would find out. He'll be called out to the scene."

"You shot your own partner?" My stomach boiled, bucking at the thought.

"I had to get rid of Sloan and the guy you've been hanging out with. Damn, who would have thought somebody your age would have a boyfriend?"

I struggled to come up with a suitable scathing reply but my brain was frozen. "I wish he was here now," I whispered. "He'd know what to do."

"Do you want me to call Bill?" Tim said in my ear.

"I wish I could talk to him," I repeated. "He'll be worried when he finds out I'm gone."

"Oh, wait," Tim whispered. "I'll call him and have him call you. I'll—I don't have his number. Does he have a cell phone?"

I longed to scream but settled for a sigh. I didn't know Bill's number, and even if I did, there was no way I could relay it. What could I do, recite a phone number and not expect to be noticed? "What's your name?" I asked. "I don't even know who you are."

"You don't know me. I'm just a cop." The man tapped the steering wheel then said softly, "It's one thing to kill Jimmy Van in the heat of the moment. It's another to kill a woman in cold blood. I have to draw the line somewhere. If I hurt you, no way will Sal let it die down."

He was trying to convince himself again. It was unnerving.

"I've got his phone number," Tim said excitedly. "When he dropped his credit card receipt the other night and I found it, I knew it was a sign. So I did some research on him. I've got his phone number. I'm sure of it. I'll call him and have him call you." The buzz in my ear went silent.

Unmindful of my hidden conversation, my captor said, "Sloan is the big fly in the ointment. Sloan might not let Sal off the hook. He might get pissy. Now *him* I could kill." He glanced back at me and smiled grimly. "I haven't come this far to back out now."

The drugs must be fogging my brain. Then I realized what Tim had said. Had he tried the credit card fraud on Bill? I tried to imagine sick Tim, driving down the highway as he tried to retrieve a cell phone number, dial it, and talk to Bill.

All I could visualize was an accident.

"Look, just let me go," I said desperately. "I can't identify you. I haven't gotten a good look at you."

"They know. Martin knew. He was watching me. You're the nail in the coffin."

I didn't like the sound of that.

"I wasn't ready to move this fast, but I knew something was up this afternoon when Martin said he had to meet somebody and I went with him. I checked with some people and they mentioned an informal line-up. Then it all fell into place."

"How did you know I'd be at the golf tournament?"

"Sloan."

"I don't believe you. Marcus Sloan wouldn't be in cahoots with you." I laid my head against the window but the cold air sent a lancing shot of agony through my neck. I straightened as much as I was able.

The man laughed harshly. "He wasn't. But he did tell Martin where he was going. I told a loser guy to get there and call me if you showed up."

"The loser..." Tim. That must be who he meant. This was the cop who'd contacted Tim, the one who had Tim so worried. I closed my eyes, trying to will my beleaguered brain to work. But the drug was still making me hazy and I couldn't seem to put together a coherent thought.

"He was scared enough to do what I told him, but he chickened out when it came to getting you out of the building. The little weasel," the man added.

"So you got that slut Crystal to help you instead. What happened—did Tim introduce you to her?"

"She was anxious to help. It was the whole woman scorned thing."

"Woman scorned?" I started to argue this description but my phone thumped my hip. I pressed my head against the door handle, activating the answer button.

"I just told her I was a cop and I needed her help to get you away from Manion. She came up with the idea of the so-called attempted rape."

"That bitch," I spat.

"Threemie?"

I almost wept with relief. It was Bill.

"Hang on. I'm putting you on speaker phone," he said.

I heard the sound of traffic and a horn honking. "Where are we?" I asked, praying Bill would get the hint. I peered out the window. "Exit 19? We're on the interstate? There's nothing out here but farms."

"Your friend Steven saw him drag you out of the bar," I heard Sloan say in the background. "He got the license plate number. It's Bobby Fowler's car."

"Bo—" I stopped myself in time. The man who was driving didn't notice.

"I told you. We're going to meet some friends of mine." The car slowed and we ascended a hill then stopped.

"It's so dark." I caught a glimpse of a sign. "Highway 3? Where does that go?"

"Did you get us some help?" I heard Bill ask.

"Yeah. But we don't want to push him into doing something."

"He's already done something," Bill snapped. "He's not getting away with this."

"With what?" Bill asked.

*Yeah,* I thought. *With what?*

"Fowler's got a lot of friends in the Hmong community," Sloan said. His voice faded in and out, as though he was moving away from the phone. "He doesn't know he's being followed. He's taking his time."

"So are you," I said.

"What?" The man took a right turn, using the action to glance back at me.

I struggled to sit more upright, nearly dislodging the phone set from my ear in the process. "So are you taking me out of the country?"

"I told you already. I've got friends who will handle it. I'm just going to hand you off."

I heard Sloan say, "Shit. Farms. That's all we need. A lot of empty country."

I peered out my window. We were on one of the many county roads crisscrossing Minnesota, two-lane blacktop running in straight lines east and west, north and south.

I heard Bill say, "Why aren't you setting up road blocks? Why aren't there a bunch of squad cars out here with sirens blaring?"

I strained to hear Sloan's reply, but only caught part of it. "This is...just a simple kidnapping. We're...he'll lead us to the rest of the people involved..."

"And put Threemie in danger while he does?" Bill's voice was ominously low.

"We're almost there," the man—Bobby Fowler—said.

"Jimmy Vann was killed because...young kids have...lives ruined because of him and his buddies. We'd like to stop it."

"Not at the expense of Threemie's life."

I silently applauded Bill's protest but knew it was meaningless. If the cops could break up a prostitution ring, I was sure they'd be willing to put my life at risk. I hazarded a look behind me. A car was in the distance, the headlights stabbing through the darkness.

"Threemie, we're on the interstate behind you. We'll catch up."

If they were still on the interstate, they were far

behind us. I swallowed the nausea that threatened. "Did you expect a fight to break out in the bar?"

The man shook his head, a shadowy movement in the dark. "Just a lucky break."

"Sloan got back and we took off after you as fast as we could," Bill was saying in my ear. "Tim called me. He said he was following you. Do you see him?"

"Maybe," I said.

"Maybe what?" Fowler asked.

"Maybe it wasn't as lucky as you thought."

He looked at me in the rear view mirror. I shifted position, ducking my head slightly until I was sure the headset was in the shadows. "We'll see." He abruptly jerked the wheel and we slid on the gravel of a side road.

"Hey, be careful," I said, bouncing painfully off the door handle. "What is this? Where are we? What's that? It looks like construction equipment."

"Construction site, highway 3," Sloan said in the background. He must have been talking into another phone.

"Threemie, we're on the way."

The phone went suddenly silent.

Chapter 16

Fowler turned off the car lights and we were plunged into a farm-dark night. "We'll go off the road," I said, peering at the dense blackness surrounding us.

The car dipped and swayed. Fowler bent over the steering wheel, staring intently ahead, the parking lights of the car the only brightness in the suffocating dark. The car inched forward and I saw several buildings rise around us like monoliths in the night. I suddenly realized where we were: it was a new office park. They were springing up all over the metro area. I had no idea where this was, but it was probably only ten or fifteen miles from the southernmost suburb.

The car slid on the snow-topped gravel, a couple of times getting close to the ditch. After several minutes, we rounded a corner and saw...nothing.

"Where are they?" Fowler sounded like he was talking out loud to himself. He stopped the car, clinging to the steering wheel then punched the power button for his window. Cold air flooded the car. He let up on the brake and we meandered forward again.

There was a smell of vegetation on the air and a dry smell of...grain or plants. I saw stubbly silhouettes out the front windshield and realized a cornfield was just ahead of us. The construction site was probably cut out of a farm field. The wind had picked up and the dry cornstalks of last year's crop were rustling in the field nearby. The cold from the open window made me shiver but I was also hot, maybe from the drug. It was an odd, schizophrenic feeling.

Fowler pulled up to a building, the weak headlights showing a gaping opening where a door would someday be. "We're on foot from here on in." He reached up and turned off the interior light then opened the car door. I barely had time to straighten up before he jerked my door open and dragged me out by the arms.

I could see the shape of a tall building directly ahead of me. Dim security lighting shone inside the structure while on the other side was a brighter yard light. Two other buildings were in the distance, but the lighting was poor and I couldn't tell how large they were.

I stumbled on the rutted, frozen ground as Fowler dragged me to my feet. "Come on. Just a little further."

"Until what?" I tried to tug against the grip holding me but only succeeded in tripping over clods of frozen dirt. By the time I found my balance again, I was inside the building, skidding on the raw wooden floor. "Where are we? Where are you taking me?"

"Come on. Go there, down that hall." He shoved me forward.

Pain flared in my head and I was suddenly dizzy. "I can't," I said, leaning against a doorframe. I looked around, but my vision was blurring. The walls were bare joists with the outlines of doorways at set intervals. I turned to Fowler. "I can't." I started to sag downward, nausea making my legs buckle.

"Damn it." His voice faded.

**** 

*Well, this just sucks*, I thought groggily. I raised my head and a piercing headache shot through my brain. "Ow." I squinted, trying to see where I was. *Not only am I not with Bill but I'm cold and alone. And...*"It smells bad," I said loudly. To my surprise, my voice echoed.

"Just go to sleep."

I blinked. I was sitting on the floor in a small room—a very dirty, smelly, cold small room. The floor was dusty and had sharp, crumbly sand on it. It sparkled in the dim light on the floor next to me. I stared at the flickering flashlight illuminating my space. "It's too cold to sleep."

"Look, this didn't work out the way I planned." Whoever was speaking sounded apologetic and angry. No, I decided. Defensive. He sounded defensive.

I looked for the voice but couldn't find it. Was it Fowler? It was hard to tell, the sound seemed to be echoing. The voice appeared to be coming from beneath me, which made little sense. I wiggled on the floor, trying to get comfortable. My ankles were tied together. I tugged my legs, but they wouldn't come apart.

I decided to try reasoning. "I'm sorry about that but I'm cold." Maybe if I were reasonable, the voice would be reasonable and get me some heat.

"I was supposed to meet some people here but they haven't showed up. So you just wait. When they get here, you'll be nice and warm." The voice faded slightly and sounded worried. "Where are those guys? They're supposed to be here. They'll show up. They've never let me down in all these years we've worked together. They just got delayed..."

"Look, I appreciate the fact you're waiting for someone but I need some help here."

"No one knows about this place but me and the guys. Every time we brought the kids in, we used a different construction site. Nobody knows. I'm sure of it."

He didn't sound sure of it. He didn't sound confident at all. I pushed my worry about it aside and focused on the words that mattered: *Nobody knows about this place but me.* I didn't like the sound of that.

"You won't be alone for long. They'll take care of you."

The voice sounded as though it was going away. "Hello?" I called. "I'm cold now. I don't want to wait." My hands were frozen. I peered down at my hands and the thin white cord binding them together then I focused on the walls. What I saw made my heart stutter.

"I'm in an elevator."

The control panel on the wall was very small, with only five buttons. I could barely see them in the flickering light. I fought the panic that threatened. Stand up. I needed to stand up. If I could stand up, I could get to the control panel and press the Open button. That was reasonable. I needed a plan. I needed to stand up.

With laborious care I wiggled onto one side, cocked my legs, rolled onto my front, and managed to prop myself up on my bound arms. "Okay, good." I stared at the grimy floor. Why was the floor so dirty? Why didn't it have carpet? Why wasn't there any heat? I realized I was only wearing my Bombshell sweatshirt and jeans—no coat, mittens, or hat. Dim memory came back to me. I was grabbed out of the bar without any coat or hat. I struggled upward. No wonder I was cold. I leaned against the wall, panting from my exertions. The wall was cold, too. The floor and walls were cold. Shit, the *air* was cold.

I lurched for the control panel, landing with a solid thud in the corner, still propped up by the wall. I flayed for the buttons, punching several at random.

Nothing happened.

Panic threatened again. My plan wasn't working. "Okay. Time for a new plan. Don't panic. Figure this out." My head was throbbing and my throat was so dry I could barely talk. "Hello?" I called out, wondering if I imagined the earlier voice. "Hello?"

My voice echoed. The flashlight flickered and dimmed. I lunged for it, landing hard on my knees, feeling my jeans tear. I fumbled for the switch as it went out.

Darkness closed around me.

"Well, shit."

My voice echoed in the cold air.

The phone on my waist thumped. I sagged against the wall, pressing my bound hands against my ear. "What?"

"I'm here. That son of a bitch lied to me."

Dear God, it was Tim again.

"I hid my car and followed Fowler. You looked sick. Are you okay?"

"No, I'm not okay," I managed to croak. "I'm in an elevator."

"That son of a bitch lied. This is all wrong."

"No shit. Look, I'm in an elevator. Can you find me?"

"I'm just coming in the building. Hold on, I'll—"

I held my breath. "Tim?"

The line was dead.

"Damn!" I struggled to sit upright, fighting the panic the small, damp, claustrophobic space inspired in me. This was nothing like the other elevator, the one in California. That one was bright and clean. It had pastel walls and nice carpet. It had a ventilation system. It didn't smell moldy and...I sniffed. Pissy. That other elevator was warm and clean and bright. This one was cold. It creaked. It made noises when the wind moved.

*I can't believe this is happening,* I thought, clawing my way up the side of the elevator and staggering to my feet. I made my way, hopping, to the corner and huddled in its comforting confines. That damn Marcus Sloan. Some bodyguard he was. *I was supposed to play golf then go home with Bill and make love all night. This isn't fair! I find a big handsome hunk of man and some asshole kidnaps me! Damn Marcus Sloan! What kind of a cop is he?*

I ached to hit somebody. Unfortunately, my hands were tied and all I could do was thump against the unmoving elevator doors. I glared around the dark space. Small details became clearer: a grill in the ceiling above me, a faint vertical light where the doors met, and a reflection bouncing off the flashlight, still on the floor. When I saw Sloan again, I would read him the riot act. I pushed away from the wall, hopping to the door again.

The elevator door refused to budge even when I got my fingers into the narrow little groove. I sniffled then rubbed my face on my sweatshirt sleeve. "I can't believe this. I just meet the guy of my dreams, I'm having great sex, and the time of my life. I can't die here." I pressed against the cold dark walls, anger overcoming my fear.

"IT'S NOT FAIR!!!!"

I screamed so loud I thought I might have ruptured something. I sagged in the corner, exhausted, tears coursing down my cheeks.

"Threemie?" someone shouted.

Bill? I hopped to the doors, pressing my face against the meager crack. "Bill?" My voice was raw and came out in a croak. I prepared to shout again then stopped. What if the round-faced man was still there? If I called out, I'd give away Bill's location. "Bill," I whispered. I looked around my dark space and spied the flashlight. I pounced on it and began tapping.

Three quick taps; pause; three taps; pause; three quick taps. I prayed I was remembering my Girl Scout training correctly.

"Threemie?"

I wondered if he heard the repetitive tapping or if he'd chalked it up to noise caused by the wind. I tried to visualize the space where he'd be. If the elevator lobby was as unfinished as the rest of the office space I glimpsed, he might not even notice the elevator shaft in the mess of the construction.

"Threemie?"

I tapped again.

"Threemie?" His voice was louder now, near but coming from below me.

"In here." I sagged against the wall, relief making me weak.

"Hey, I found you."

"Yeah, how about that? I'm stuck, I think."

"Not to worry. I'm here, we'll figure out something."

"Where's Sloan? I'm going to give him a piece of my mind when I see him."

"He's busy, I think. We split up when we came into the building."

"Did you see Tim?"

"Tim who? Listen, Threemie—the elevator isn't moving."

"I know. I'm stuck. Tim McIntyre. He called me. He said he was here."

"Where?"

"Here somewhere. I don't know."

"Where are you? Can you tell?"

"I woke up in here. I'm tied up."

"You sound at least one floor, maybe two, above me. How many floors are on the control panel?"

"I think five." I touched the buttons. "Yeah. Five, I think."

"I'm coming upstairs."

"Hey, Bill?"

"What?"

"I'm sort of afraid of elevators. And dark small spaces. And..." I struggled against a sob, "...and falling."

Something pounded the door below me. I jumped back, afraid I was falling. "Sorry. That was me. Look, I'm on my way, Threemie. Don't worry about it."

"I am. Worrying, that is." My voice came out small and thin.

"Threemie?"

"Yeah?"

"I'm a mechanic, honey. I can fix anything."

I laughed shakily. "Yeah, that's right. You're a mechanic. I knew there was a reason I wanted to marry you. You can fix anything."

"You keep thinking about it. I'm coming up in the stairwell so I can figure out where you are. I'll see you in a few minutes."

"Okay. Hurry, please? I'm cold. I don't have a coat."

The phone in my ear suddenly crackled to life. I heard rustling sounds then voices, as though from far away. Had Tim stuck the phone in his pocket? Was he holding it down and away, so it wasn't seen?

"You son of a bitch," Marcus Sloan said. "You killed Jimmy Vann."

"It was an accident. It just happened."

Holy shit. Sloan was confronting the round-faced man. Was Tim there?

"What happened, Bobby?" Sloan asked.

"Drop your gun," Fowler said. "No way am I

going to prison. Drop it."

I heard a sound like something falling hollowly. Had Sloan tossed his gun down? "They know about you," Sloan said. "This won't help you, Bobby. They suspected you."

"I wondered. Her?"

"She remembered you."

"Damn. I was afraid of that."

"We were just waiting to see what you did. She picked you out of an informal line-up this afternoon. Sal got a court order and they're searching your financial records now. It's over, Bobby. It's done."

There was a long pause and I wondered what was happening. Where was Bill? Where was Tim? Where the hell were Marcus Sloan and Bobby Fowler?

"McIntyre?" Sloan asked.

I jerked so hard I almost dislodged the headset from my ear. Tim was there?

"I didn't know what was going on. He lied to me." Tim coughed, a terrible, rasping noise that made my chest ache just to hear it.

"He lied to everybody," Sloan said. "You're not alone. What now?"

"Now you both go outside."

I could almost see Fowler, holding a gun and gesturing with it.

"It won't help you to get rid of us," Sloan said. "They know about you."

"This didn't work out the way I planned."

I strained to hear, the silence of the elevator shaft actually helping. I heard footsteps then someone shouted. "Get down! Move!"

There was a crashing sound then a scuffling noise, like the phone had dropped onto drywall or boards. I heard shouts.

Then I heard a gunshot. It was so loud I jerked back, thinking it was next to me.

I heard more shouts and scuffling then the horrible sound of something hard hitting something soft—like a board hitting someone's head or a metal pipe connecting with a skull.

"Tim? Are you okay? Tim?" I whispered frantically.

"I'm here," Bill said.

I lunged for the cold metal doors of the elevator. "Hey, I'm here, too. How about that? Now if we could just get these doors open, we could be here together."

"I'll see what I can do." I heard him try to pry the doors open with his hands but they didn't budge.

"I'll find something," he said. "Hang on. There's a bunch of construction stuff here. Maybe there are some tools or something." There was a long pause and I heard metal pipes, boards, and other things being shoved around. "Threemie?"

"Yeah, I'm still here."

"Stand back, okay? I'm going to pry around a bit on the door."

"You go, boy."

I slid back, away from the doors, and watched breathlessly. "Tim?" I whispered. "Are you still there? What's happening?"

All I got back was static. I stared at the door, praying that it would open. It did, but in small increments. Light started to filter into my elevator prison, at first just a small glow then finally more brightness as Bill wedged in pieces of board and pipe. The opening widened an inch at a time. I got down on the floor and peered out, my face level with his. Behind him, I saw construction materials and what looked like a doorframe. "Hey. How did you get here?"

"We followed you." He smiled at me but I could see his fear in his eyes.

"We?"

"Marcus Sloan and me."

"Where is he? I want to give him a piece of my mind about his security arrangements." Then I remembered the gunshot. "Shit. I hope he's okay. If he's okay, I'm going to yell at him."

"I'm not sure. I'm going to get you out."

"I'm ready. Actually, I'm more than ready. I'm lying on the floor now. Obviously we have a problem here."

He nodded. "I can pry these doors open some more and you can slip out."

I shook my head. "I'd rather not. What if the elevator jerks or something? Can't you make the elevator move?"

Bill started to argue with me but he must have seen my terrified look. I was trembling, too. It might have been fear, shock, or the cold, but I'm sure I looked like I was at the end of my rope.

"I'll have to go upstairs and check the machinery. There's usually a machine room on the roof."

I wiggled my hands into the crack of the door. "Okay."

Bill grasped my fingers, giving me a reassuring tug. "I'll just be right above you. I'll get you out."

"Well, you'd better. I've decided the marriage thing is a good idea. Retirement is looking good right now."

"Then I'd better get you out of there before you change your mind." He smiled confidently. "Don't worry. I'll fix it." He released my fingers and disappeared from sight.

I huddled back on the floor, peering out the crack at the dusty debris outside. I was about four feet above floor level, far enough that it was a scary drop to try to slither out. I laid my head on the cold floor and tried to still my shivering.

"You okay?"

The voices crackled in my ear. It sounded like

Sloan.

"Yeah." I heard a rasping, choking cough. It was Tim. "Fine." He sounded like death but I was surprised he was even still standing.

"Check on Manion. And find some lights. We need lights."

*No shit,* I thought, shivering. I huddled in the light that came in through the narrow opening as though it would provide heat, too. No such luck. *Find us some lights, some power, and some more damn cops.*

"Lights I can do. I saw a control panel." Tim coughed again. "I'll do what I can." I heard footsteps running.

"You son of a bitch." Sloan's hoarse voice was muted. "I can't believe you shot me, Fowler."

I winced. Sloan was injured? Had Tim left the phone behind? What the hell was happening?

"Jesus, you almost killed me, Sloan. What did you hit me with?"

"I should have hit you harder. Don't get up, Fowler."

I heard a wailing in the distance. Sirens? Was help really on the way? I sat up straighter, but the headset almost dropped out of my ear so I sank back to the floor. It was sirens. I could hear them clearly now. They were closer.

"Don't!" Sloan shouted.

This time the gunshot surprised me so much I did tip back, the headset slipping off my ear and falling with a clatter to the floor outside the elevator.

Chapter 17

Brilliant light flared above me. "Hey! The lights are on! It's a start!" I called out.

Bill shouted down from above. "The problem must be in the control box, Threemie. I can't find anything wrong up here. I'm coming down."

I heard a hollow, echoing sound from the stairway on my right. "Tim? Is that you?"

"Is Sloan okay?" I heard Bill ask.

"I'm not sure. Need help?" Tim's voice wheezed painfully.

"Yeah. She's stuck in the elevator. I looked at the motor housing and didn't see anything wrong. I think it must be in the control panel."

I stared out the small crack in the doors, edging as far as I could to the left so I could peer to the right, where the stairwell door was located. I saw Bill come in, then behind him I saw Tim McIntyre stagger out, using the wall for support until they got to the elevator. He eyed the building products propping open the door. "Ingenious," he muttered. He peered inside the car and saw me looking out at him.

"Did you turn on the lights?" I asked.

Tim leaned against the wall as a hacking fit took him. I waited until he'd finished coughing then said, "Thanks for the lights."

Tim smiled. "It's the least I could do. Let's get you unstuck." He considered Bill, who was pacing the area looking for tools. He joined him near a pile of construction debris near the elevator. "Can you prop it open?" he asked, jerking a thumb to the elevator door.

Bill paused. "She's afraid to jump out," he said in a low voice.

"Yes, she is," I chimed in. "Sorry, but I am."

"Can't blame you," Tim said, looking at the elevator car. "But I can jump in." He looked from me to Bill. "I know electrical better than you."

I smiled at him, my face pressed against the floor. "You'd do that?"

Tim nodded. "Better do it soon, though. I'm wearing out."

Bill gave him an assessing look. "Can you do it?"

"Yeah." Tim coughed again but this time it didn't last as long. He rubbed his chest then turned to Bill, his thin face sallow in the bright lights. "Let's do it."

Bill hesitated, looking up at me as I gestured him closer.

"What's the problem?" I whispered.

Bill looked at Tim, who was sagged against the wall. "I checked the motor up above and everything looked fine. So it must be something wrong in the control box."

I glanced upward at the control box. "It looks okay. But what do I know? I don't know a wrench from a hammer." I regarded Tim, gesturing Bill closer. "Do we trust him?" I whispered, my face pressed hard against the small crack in the elevator doors.

"We don't have much choice. Tim's an electrical

guy. I'm mechanical."

I regarded him for a long moment. "You're pretty damn electrical as far as I'm concerned," I whispered. "And not mechanical at all. But I see the problem. So what do we do?"

"I'm going to join you," Tim said, pushing away from the wall. "Bill the weightlifter is going to get these doors open and I'm coming up."

"Oh." I looked at Bill. "Can you do it?"

Bill nodded. "He's thin. We'll manage it." He pulled Tim aside. "It'll be tricky. I need something to wedge in there and you need something to climb on."

Tim pointed to a pile of scrap lumber, mostly two-by-fours with the longest almost six feet long. "You get it open two feet and jam one into the top, in the rail at the top of the door."

"What about you?" Bill asked, dragging over the lumber.

"I'll figure out something." He helped Bill wedge in the lumber at an angle, prying open the doors until they could jam the larger boards into the railing housing the track for the opening. Bill leaned his shoulders against one side and put his leg up on the other door. It was a tight fit but he wedged himself in.

Tim looked down at Bill then up at me. "Catch me." Then he stepped on Bill's outstretched thigh to scramble up into the elevator car. I tugged Tim upward, leaning back and pulling with all my might. Tim scraped his way into the car, just clearing the doors when the lumber holding them open snapped.

Bill scrambled back out of the way as the doors slammed shut on Tim and me.

I lunged for the doors. "Bill!"

Tim rolled against the far wall as the elevator lurched. I was thrown off balance, landing in a pile near him. The elevator dropped several feet then stopped with a teeth-rattling *thunk*. I huddled in the corner, bruised and shaken. "Damn, what happened?" I rolled awkwardly onto my knees, scrabbling to the doors and pounding on them. "Bill?" I looked at Tim, who was rubbing his forehead. "Is he okay? What happened?"

"I don't know. The best thing we can do for him is get this car stabilized."

I stared at the closed doors, my fear making me sick. Bill could be hurt. He could be trapped in the doors. He could be—I took a deep, long breath, willing myself to calm. "Okay," I said, turning to Tim. "What do we do?"

"Good You're not going weepy on me. I need help. Get me on my feet and prop me up." He leaned his head back against the wall of the elevator, shivering.

I rolled to one wall, inching my way upward until I was fully upright. That was when he saw the cords on my hands and ankles. "I've got a knife." He dug into his jeans pockets, emptying out spare change, a wadded up piece of paper, and his keys. He fumbled for the Swiss Army knife dangling from the keychain. "Move over here," he said, tapping the floor near him. "I'll get your ankles first."

I hopped over to him and watched as he pulled out the knife attachment. "That's one of those knife things. I should get one. If I'd had it, I wouldn't be in this mess."

"Women don't like to carry things in their pockets," Tim said as he sawed at the cords. "You'd probably never carry it if you had one."

"I'd put it in my purse. I'd carry it."

"And where's your purse?" Tim asked, folding the knife back into the base unit. "Help me up here, okay?"

I glared at him but helped him to his feet. He opened the knife again, sawing at the cords binding my wrists. "Let's check the control box," he said as the last bit of rope fell to the floor. He folded up the blade then pulled out the can opener attachment.

"I always wondered how that worked." I watched as he used the flat end of the opener to unwind the screws holding the panel's face in place. "I thought there was a little screwdriver thing you could use."

Tim lowered the metal faceplate to look at the mass of wiring behind it. "There is." He studied the wires snaking around the inside of the small box, tugging out a handful of blue, red, green, yellow, and black wires.

I hovered nearby. "We should hurry. Bill might be hurt. We should hurry and get the doors open."

Tim nodded. "Yeah, we should." He opened the knife again to pull out the small blade. With a grimace, he sorted through the mass of wiring and isolated two of them, which he cut. They sparked and flared.

"What are you doing?" I demanded, coughing at the acrid fumes.

"Shorting out the wiring so I can rewire it." Tim put the blade away, tugging out the cap lifter on the knife to quickly strip the wires. Then he twisted two other wires together. The lights flickered. He cursed and undid the wiring then screwed two others together. I watched the doors as they slowly inched apart.

As soon as they were wide enough, I leaned my shoulders into the space and looked out. The floor of the car was now several feet below the level of the floor. I saw Bill sprawled in a pile of debris not far away, unmoving. "Bill!" I scrambled up the side of the elevator onto the floor of the foyer, landing hard on my stomach. I tucked my legs out of the elevator then scrambled across the rough floor on hands and knees, landing with a plop near Bill, who lay still and pale in a tangle of sheetrock, drywall and pipes.

I leaned over him, scanning his body quickly. No

blood. That was good. No, wait—there was some blood, on the bruise from the car accident. The car accident. Damn, I'd forgotten all about it. My attention snapped back to the elevator and Tim McIntyre. "Are you okay?" I called back.

He waved at me. "I've got the manual override working. I'll go down to the ground floor and get help. Is he okay? What do we need?"

I turned back to Bill to find him regarding me with those dark blue eyes. "He's fine," Bill said. "Just got knocked on my ass."

"He's fine," I called back. "We're both fine."

"I'll get help and be right back," Tim said. The inner doors closed and the elevator dropped slowly from sight. The outer doors remained open several feet.

"You scared the hell out of me," I said, touching Bill's face. "Are you sure you're okay?"

He nodded then winced. "I've got a few more bruises but I'm okay. When the wood snapped, I rolled out of there. I got clipped by some of the debris."

I glanced around when I heard footsteps in the stairwell. "I hope that's Sloan," I said, getting to my knees. "It's about time my lousy bodyguard showed up, I'm going to—"

Bobby Fowler rushed out of the stairwell and came at us, carrying a gun. I jumped to my feet and behind me Bill struggled upright, one hand holding his ribs. "What the hell are you doing here?" I demanded, glaring at Fowler.

He glared back, shooting a quick glance around the small foyer. "I'm just passing through, looking for a way out of here to avoid the mess out front."

"Out front?" I suddenly realized there was a lot of noise and lights bouncing off the ceilings. "Police?"

Fowler started to edge past me. Then he hesitated. I could almost see the wheels turning in his mind: *hostages. Should I take hostages?* I reached down to pick up a short length of pipe.

"No you don't," I said, advancing on him and raising the pipe. "Not again."

Startled, Fowler backed up a step. It was one step too many. The open outer doors of the elevator shaft were directly behind him. Before he could catch his balance, he toppled backwards, out of sight.

****

I pushed away the paramedic who was attempting to look at my wrists. "I'm fine. You should look at Bill. He was in a car accident and—"

The paramedic gently shoved me back onto the gurney. "You need stitches in your knee."

We were in the "lobby" of the building. What had been empty space was now full of paramedics, gurneys, and policemen. One gurney had just been whisked away, carrying Marcus Sloan. Another held Tim McIntyre, looking wan and exhausted. I sat on another one and Bobby Fowler was being wheeled past on yet another gurney.

I looked in surprise at my torn jeans and the gaping, bloody wound. "Wow. When did I do that?"

"Choose," Bill said, walking over to stand next to me. "When you fell down when the flashlight went out? When the elevator lurched? When you jumped out to help me?" He stared down at me, a bright white bandage covering the stitches on his face. He'd heard my entire story several times as I babbled it to the police. "You need to get it healed, though. We've got a date for a wedding and a honeymoon and—" He bent over and whispered, "I have plans for those knees, honey. I like it when the girl is on top sometimes. You need to get healed."

"I didn't think about that." I turned to the EMT. "Let's get those stitches done."

Bill laughed but sobered when he saw the

ambulance outside pull away. "How's Sloan?" he asked the police captain who was standing nearby.

"Bad," the man introduced as Captain Salisbury said. "Touch and go." He glowered at the gurney trundling past, carrying Bobby Fowler. "That bastard got off with broken legs, a concussion and broken ribs. Sometimes life ain't fair."

"Sloan is tough," Bill said. "He'll be okay. I'm sure of it."

I looked up at Bill. "I hope so." I squeezed his hand.

"Thanks to you we've broken up a prostitution ring," Salisbury said, turning back to me. "I can't believe Bobby was so stupid. If he'd just let you alone, we wouldn't have had anything on him."

"But I could identify him," I protested, wincing as the EMT dabbed disinfectant on my wrists where the cords had bit into my skin.

"You could place him in the garage," the captain pointed out. "It might have been enough to get us a search warrant. Might not have been, though. We didn't have anything else on him, just suspicions."

"How's his partner?" Bill asked. "Sloan mentioned the guy had been shot."

"Recovering. Marcus said Fowler set up Martin." He shook his head. "We're just starting to get a handle on it, but it looks like Bobby had a nice financial portfolio. He's been pulling this shit for years."

"He was lucky," I said.

Bill took my hand and gave it a shake. "You need to go to the hospital to get those stitches. I'll follow and meet you there."

I watched as Tim McIntyre was wheeled past. He looked very pale and his eyes were closed. "He and Crystal were in cahoots, weren't they?"

Bill smoothed my hair back from my bruised forehead. "Yeah, they were."

I gestured him closer. "We still need to discuss that woman and the memories she's left behind."

He smiled down at me, his eyes dark and loving. "Nah. We just need to make a bunch of new memories so I don't have room for the old ones. We'll replace all our old memories, of her and of your ex. Deal?"

"Deal."

He kissed me gently. "Now get to the hospital and get those stitches taken care of so I can take you home. Tonight's my night to play nurse for you."

****

It was a lovely early spring day in mid-April. It hadn't snowed for almost two weeks and the slush had melted off the roadways. Bill declared the weather was fine enough for a drive in the park. We opened the doors on the workshop then Bill started up the Mustang. Just as we were getting ready to drive out into the street, Marcus Sloan pulled up.

"Taking it out for a drive?" he asked as he got out of his battered Honda and came to stand next to the car.

Bill smiled. "You're looking good. Did the doctor give you permission to leave the house?" As it turned out, Sloan had been wounded twice. The first one got him in the arm but the second gunshot wound occurred when Marcus and Bobby Fowler grappled for the gun. That bullet narrowly missed puncturing Sloan's lung. He'd been in surgery for hours and had been released from the hospital just the week before.

"What the doctor doesn't know won't hurt him." Sloan leaned on the car and peered in at me. "Hey there."

"Hey, Detective. How's it going?"

"Pretty good. I suppose you're busy getting ready for the wedding."

I shook my head. "Nah. I made Steven handle everything. He and the folks from work are planning a real extravaganza. I can't wait." I beamed him a million watt smile.

"I just thought you'd like to know—Bobby Fowler is going to be fit enough to stand trial in a month. So make sure you're back from the honeymoon by then."

Bill fed some gas to the Mustang, which responded with a throaty purr. "We will. How much lounging on a beach can two people do?"

Sloan and I exchanged bemused glances. "A lot," he said. "Oh, and Tim McIntyre—I talked to him, too. Turns out his doctor had some good news for him. His cancer is going into remission with a new drug treatment they're doing." He looked at Bill. "That was big of you. I still say you should have pressed charges."

I agreed. "I know he helped us in the end, but I still have a hard time forgiving him."

"Can't blame you," Marcus said. "He's got a part-time job at the hospital, from what I hear. At least it'll keep him busy."

I covered Bill's hand on the gearshift. "Maybe I'll try to contact him sometime, just to see how he's doing. Later. After we get home. Right now we've got a test drive to do."

Sloan tapped the roof of the convertible and stepped back. "Have fun, you two. Don't do anything I wouldn't do."

"That covers a lot of ground," I called out. "See you later."

Bill turned to me. "I was thinking we might take a drive through the park. It's such a nice, sunny day."

I leaned back against the leather upholstery. "That sounds like fun." I gave him a mischievous smile. "If you're feeling adventurous, I could recreate some of my Mustang memories for you."

He raised an eyebrow. "That sounds like a deal."

An hour later, he discovered the back seat of a 1966 Ford Mustang convertible was indeed big enough, because he was certainly motivated.

And I sure was agile.

## A word about the author...

I was born in a small town in Iowa and have traveled extensively in the U.S. and overseas, finally ending up back in the Midwest, where I'm married to a glass artist who spends a lot of time in the studio making amazingly beautiful things. We have assorted animals who live with us and who make regular appearances in my books under various pseudonyms. (They know who they are.)

In 2003, I read my first romance novel and immediately decided this was the genre for me. But there was a problem: the books I read all featured young heroines, interested in starting a family and having babies. So I started writing romantic suspense (with an occasional side trip into paranormal fantasy) about older women, with some age on 'em, who are interested in men and sex and having a good relationship (which may or may not include a marriage). I hope you enjoy reading about them as much as I enjoy writing about them.

Contact JL at jaye@jayellwilson.com
Visit JL at www.jayellwilson.com

Thank you for purchasing
this Wild Rose Press publication.
For other wonderful stories of romance,
please visit our on-line bookstore at
www.thewildrosepress.com.

For questions or more information,
contact us at
info@thewildrosepress.com.

The Wild Rose Press
www.TheWildRosePress.com